CW00401496

TARRY THE GRINDING

a story by

Antony Stone

CHAPTER ONE

There were nightmares left out in the sky to make trouble. One had already entered Frederik's head. That could not have been easy because his brain was already crammed with confusion, irritation and frustration. As if life was not enough, there was death to be considered and though information on how to cope with the first was fulsome to the point of saturation, hard evidence regarding the latter seemed impossible to obtain. Those who said it was the end of everything were no less convinced than those who declared it to be just the beginning; though Frederik could not escape the thought that as a beginning (meaning as it must that things had not started yet) what is the bit we are in right now.

Most of the time he was faithful to the belief of non-belief; that after death there is nothing. This conviction had been planted early by his uncle, the black sheep of the family, a communist whose other beliefs included a policy of ripping the innards out of any public telephone kiosk, which was not working properly. 'There will be no malfunction in the perfect communist state,' hence, no misfortune; no misalignment of mind, body, or disposition. No wankers.

Frederik would never make it in the perfect communist state. Much more to the point, he could not make it in an imperfect capitalist state. He could not work. Not for long. Not to acceptable standards. He could talk about work, prepare for work, he could secure positions of employment, but he could not work. He was strong on fathering children (which after all is not difficult) onanism (another easy one) obsessive infatuations, daydreams and wool-gathering.

His wife could work fortunately, though reluctantly, given the circumstances and few would blame her. She was scowling as she left the house, Frederik's parents' house to which they had been forced to return after his latest career crisis and he was looking from the bedroom window to see if she was scowling. Well of course she was, who wouldn't be? Mother Teresa perhaps, but she hadn't got a husband to cope with and on second thoughts, her facial expression was very close to scowling the whole time.

Frederik settled back in bed. Not so much settle as lie rigid. He would rise in a minute or two when he had managed to calm down. Not much chance of one off the wrist, even though she had left him with the near certainty that something in his groin had stretched or burst. He could understand her not wanting to risk getting pregnant again, he could have coped with a half-fond refusal or even a 'head-ache' but did she have to make with the venom, the put-down and the emasculating uninterest. Anyway, what would it have cost her to give him a chew.

Downstairs his father's voice droned on, in what he knew would be despairing rumination about his, Frederik's, domestic and career situations; interspersed by his mother's high-pitched placatory interjections. He would give it another ten minutes; give them time to eat their toast; not due at the dole office till eleven o'clock anyway. That young piece behind the counter reminded him of his primary passion of early adolescence. 'I'm sure she was giving me the come-on. Some women respond to the lost and hopeless. Awakens a desire to mould, reform, manipulate?' That was what Prudence had been convinced she could do and was now fast losing the conviction and desire to achieve. These musings affected a lull in the stirrings in his pyjama bottoms, but a flashback to last week and anticipation of eleven this morning, reinstated progression. A few strokes wouldn't do any harm, might just blot out the sad image of last night, so stark in his head. He barely knew which excited him more, the crucifying early obsession, searing but empty as it still was, or the vague possibilities of eleven o'clock. There had been no need for her to rise and bend over to reach for his card, showing him as much breast as she could, whilst pretending not to. Must do it all the time — relieves the boredom. Suppose she had done what, released from the constraints of society and convention she might have wished; suppose she had stood calmly, spread her dress and shown him her breasts. Whoops! Steady don't want to - said I wouldn't - not convenient - and there was that top-drawer secretary type on the underground; I'm sure she knew what she was doing to me, AAaaEEeee shouldn't have. "Are you going to get up today?"

His father's voice struck as lightning must. That it had begun and ended before fully registering, did nothing to lessen Frederik's agitation. "Uuhh. Uuhh?

"I thought you were getting your breakfast."

"We'll have had luncheon if you don't get a move on."

That decided it. Now he would get up. There were no tissues handy. The hankie was a coloured one; might show. His mother did their washing. It was on the sheets as well. Prudence would notice that. Perhaps if he spread it around with the corner of the sheet where you wouldn't expect it to be he could just get away with it. Might sponge off? He crept to the bathroom; needed a 'jemmy' anyway. Why was he creeping? Guilt, that's why; but why guilty? He had read that everyone admitted to it except liars. As he reached for a flannel his mother's voice calling, "Frederik! Be careful with the clothes drier," was interrupted by the crash as it collapsed "it isn't very secure. Oh!"

What is it with women and clothes-driers (outside it was pouring, she'd be soaked getting to the bus-stop) why could they not do the washing when it could dry outside, or just hang them up in the rain; they were wet anyway.

Back in bed, Frederik's attempt at sponging was not going well. Someone had compromised the flannel with mascara. Ah yes. He had meant to rinse it thoroughly. It was just an experiment with his appearance; he had baulked at the lipstick.

"I told her to take an umbrella. She's got an umbrella. I told her to take mine. Hasn't she got an umbrella?"

His mother had entered unheralded and sideways. "Oh no, I don't need that in here." She returned the

5

vacuum cleaner to the landing and re-entered sideways, from instantaneously acquired habit. "Aren't you having breakfast? You need breakfast. What was that programme you wanted to listen to on the radio; you asked me to remind you. What are you doing? I can do that. These sheets need changing anyway. I meant to change them yesterday, but it was raining."

His mother would not notice. She would not notice the state of the sheets because she never seemed to notice anything. Frederik's mother never remarked on anything except to say that something was pretty, or 'nice' if it resulted from some act of kindliness. Perhaps Frederik's mother only pretended not to notice anything.

"I thought you were up"

"I'm not up"

"I'll come back later; you're not up."

Have to wait till it dries now, I could do with a few more minutes anyway. Why am I always tired? Fancy shouting up just at that moment, you'd think he knew. My god! Don't say he heard the bed shaking. Job only half done, nothing worse, but dare not risk another one now although I bet he has done more than his share; he never has any energy either. Might as well get up. Wait a minute; they might be going out. Better not ask. If he starts checking doors and windows, I'll know. Could be thinking what to say if they start on again about 'have you considered a different area of employment; manual labour?' — the cheeky sod. He was sneering at me, he'd seen me looking and he fancies her; but she pulled away when he squeezed past her chair. Could throw a sickie but I would have to hurry to catch morning surgery.

His asthma had been severe and now there was hayfever starting again. If the pollen count rose and he had difficulty breathing, he could call the doctor. Problem solved. Shame he had — didn't feel like looking at her now anyway. Looking lost and forlorn was one thing; pitiful and desperate was something else. His thoughts reverted inexorably to Prudence.

Though of indeterminate inception it had seemed a promising new episode; being married. Much against his expectation she had absorbed his ultimatum that he would not marry her if they did not first go away together. Somehow, subtly that had changed to, 'If you go away with me, I will marry you,' He had not noticed the slight difference between the two formulas until it was too late. He could now see that her acquiescence had rested on her confidence that her wits were sharper than his. And of course, there was the inescapable fact that she was pregnant.

She had not been very forthcoming in the sack. Much more prudence than prurience, an antiseptic sort of coolness, which he hoped would metamorphose into thermal enthusiasm within the security of marriage.

His own lack of experience was also a crucial ingredient though this hardly occurred to him. Though not quite a virgin (what is a virgin anyway) he was hardly up to grade one; failed. There had been that breathless elevating grope with a tender student of art and sex (he was her elementary exercise, quickly assimilated and abandoned) executed digitally from the rear, her response, slippery corrugated avidity, had stayed with him. And there was Paris.

Tortured, blinding frustration had impelled him to risk the unthinkable, impossible though obvious solution. H. G. Wells had owned up in his autobiography; honesty, courage, egotism? How many others? I'll tell you. Everyone. Try dating a girl with the proviso that she must pay her own way because your conscience will not allow you to feel she may be compromised. O.K. you might get an old dog. Perhaps you are an old dog yourself; have you thought of that? We are all old dogs to someone, or will be, sooner than we think.

Not quite the same thing? Alright! Hands held high in horror, bargain price moralists with a statistical bent can quote you figures in thousands or even millions of women engaged in the sex industry, each with a gross turnover (no pun intended but quite valid) of hundreds or thousands of men. That is without the rent boys and so precarious gigolos. It multiplies to a figure, which creates a credibility gap in the bar-stool Lothario's account of how he had to fight her off; together with her three friends, does it not? He may have he fought her off temporarily, but he married her in the end.

Why did it have to be Paris? What is wrong with London whores? And nowadays, it has to be Bangkok.

Paris was pukka. It was what chaps did. It was long ago, before 'zig-zig' was replaced by the more enlightened 'fucky-fucky.' And it would be the best; except it wasn't. It was all over in three seconds. "I thought she might let me have a bit of fun on the bed afterwards," he said later. Fat chance. She was back out on the boulevard before he'd had time to zipper up the perpetrator of the shamefully premature ejaculation.

Back home, he related the episode to the 'companion', "I should have had a wank first" he declared, "then I wouldn't have been so excited". Nothing more needs to be said on the subject of his sexual competence.

Then came the anxiety, recrimination and guilt. Not much guilt, but a whole lot of anxiety. He was sure he had contracted a venereal disease, syphilis for choice. Can only be cured by an extended fast, he had read in a 'health magazine'; about twenty-eight days. Conventional drug treatment only suppresses the symptoms and the dread complaint emerges years later with a spectacular display of eruptions. Frederik had no symptoms to display at the clinic, which he might have attended, had he not been too timid and ashamed.

If consensus seems within reach on the matter of Frederik's sexual conformation, I must hasten to inform that all is not yet revealed; there is more. Not a lot, but of significant content. He was open to another, shall we say persuasion, temptation, inclination? Frederik was not entirely averse to playing with the home team. The smutty experiments with his more dominant cousin could perhaps be dismissed as schoolboy prankstering, but there was at least one other episode, which took place at a flooded sandpit, where weary war-workers were wont to sunbathe and swim. Sketchily related to the 'confidant,' the scenario was one of long grass, non-seashore sand, the lone sunbather approached by a total stranger - fade-out. The narrative implied, that an erect penis, in that instance and for that individual - person - penis - did not express a preference, or the need for distinction between male and female lips.

By some quirk of disposition Frederik seemed inordinately prone to receiving the attention of individuals who subscribed to unorthodox views on sex. He acquainted himself with male persons who, while heartily propounding the glories of manhood in general and body building in particular, and advanced assurances that they were not 'queer,' nevertheless suggested they would 'help him out,' should he so wish. He appeared not totally averse to the idea.

He was also informed of, if not persuaded to the view, that adult and child sexual interaction should not be the total taboo of common perception.

That of course, in the days before the uninformed hatred of homosexuals, was replaced by hypocritical hatred of paedophiles.

In Nazi Germany you could hate Jews. In America you can hate communists. Elsewhere there is need for diversification.

Sand took centre stage several times in Frederik's life. "He ran straight down the beach into the sea." A rare, nostalgic tenderness had relaxed the worried severity of his father's face as he spoke. "He could not have been more than eighteen months old."

Sea-sand was there when Frederik was starting to live, and it was there when he began to die.

Like his father, Frederik had sandy hair before dull grey set in; and worse still, sandy eyelashes. A certain leading British film star, (leader by gross earnings? number of films appeared in? absence of moral or political persuasion?) has made no secret of his need to darken his eyelashes, so it can be admitted that that colour scheme presents difficulties, coming as it does with sunburn and freckles. Could this colour a person's disposition? And for Frederik, make him more subject to infatuations, fantasies, obsessive imprintings and transportings. The sight or recollection of a group of 'trendy yachting types' (sailing dinghy types more likely) would send his thoughts into a world to which he was sure he should belong, though he had never been there.

"We have to go. We can't wait all day." His father's shout jolted him from his reverie. "He's not sleeping again is he?"

"He was getting up when I went in half an hour ago." Voice then redirected stair-wise, but not shouting.

"The tea-pot has gone cold; you will have to make fresh. I've filled the kettle. I put the cosy on to keep it warm but if it's gone cold, you'll have to make fresh. If anyone calls, tell them I'm not in. You will have to answer the door yourself."

At last the front door was shut, the key turned and posted back through the letterbox. Frederik caught a shallow sigh, closed his eyes and sank back slowly onto and recoiled swiftly from the introversive damp patch.

"Frederik, can you hear me? I'm speaking to you through the letterbox. Your father hasn't got his key. I thought he had his key. He has his back-door key but it's bolted; his front door key. If you are out, we won't be able to get in. Can you hear me?"

Frederik could hear her. "Yes! I'll let you in."

It really was exasperating, just when he thought he could have five minutes peace. Five minutes that's all. It wasn't asking much. Now he would have to dress. Didn't want the neighbours knowing he wasn't dressed. He found one of his socks; its partner eluded him.

"You don't need to get dressed. Just put on your dressing gown. We will miss the bus if you get dressed."

Frederik's father could not trust himself to speak, but did so anyway. "Whatever is he doing? Tell him he doesn't have to - if I bend down to that letterbox I'll not straighten up again. He can pass the key back out, without opening the door."

"Your father may not be able to straighten up again. He says you can pass the key out but then you won't be able to lock the door when you go out, that is why I put it through in the first place."

"Your father says, what have you done with your own bloody - with your own key?"

"Alright I'm coming."

"He's coming now."

Frederik was grunting softly and scratching his head. "I can't see it"

"Can't see what."

"The key, I can't find it. Where did it go?"

"I don't know; I was out here. Do you know where it went Father."

Father called upon God for strength. "We have missed the bus, so it's too late to go anyhow. Just tell him to fetch my key. It is in the left pocket of my grey jacket."

"I thought you were wearing your grey jacket; it must be my eyes"

"This isn't my grey jacket it's - yes, it is - it's my grey jacket. Why didn't you tell me?"

"It must be my eyes. I didn't know you kept your key in your grey jacket. I've always liked that jacket it suits you."

"Is he going to let us in? Don't tell me he has gone back to bed again."

"I suppose he is looking for your grey jacket."

"He won't find it if I'm wearing it"

"Perhaps the key is in your grey jacket, have you checked?

"I didn't check because I thought I was wearing my other grey jacket."

Frederik coughed through the letterbox. "I can't find your grey jacket." His father, again called on the almighty for strength, took six paces towards the bus stop, turned, took two back, then turned again. Frederik's mother said, "You must have had it all the time. Isn't that funny." Frederik's father did not reply.

CHAPTER TWO

Back in the bedroom, Frederik sighed a mixture of relief and desperation. Where had that sock got to? Then he remembered. He had playfully stuffed it down the front of his underpants in an attempt to amuse Prudence. Was ever a hope more vain, a tirade more devastating.

"Oh most amusing you would do better thinking how you can bring some money into this household that is if we had a household what have you done today have you applied for any of those jobs advertised in the paper did you follow up on that one that said they wanted someone with more experience you need to keep pushing pushing you should be out scouring the streets for work anything I'm past caring what kind of work it is you are obviously incapable of holding a job you are supposed to be qualified for how did you ever qualify anyway and another thing try to acquaint yourself with a few simple facts of general knowledge you are absolutely illiterate illiterate even that so-called friend of yours knows more than you uneducated and low class as he is and don't think you are going camping this weekend because you are not like a couple of tramps oh yes that suits him with no responsibilities you've got a family have you forgotten that begging lifts talking nonsense leering at women oh yes it suits him and the way he treated Miranda the ignorant pig being flat-chested isn't a crime you should be bringing in money money you are as weak as water and don't imagine oh no I'm tired I've been working all day don't do that you are absolutely disgusting switch the light off I don't care what you do just as long as it doesn't involve me."

She continued long after his attention had been blunted to the point where a black mist descended and he was able to sleep; or possibly she fell asleep during the exposition but was able to continue. In any event she was still at it when he woke the next morning, undiminished in either volume or content, she kept going till she left the house.

Meanwhile there was a choice between an asthma attack and a gruelling encounter with the employment people. He certainly felt short of breath, but for him that was normal. When things came down to it, he was too honest to fake an attack, the whole matter of his near invalidity, was far too serious for such a thing. It was a question of degree. He knew he was incapable of coping with the world as it is, but was too proud to give in. Somewhere along the way he had been cheated and it wasn't his fault. If only, instead of doling out meagre amounts of money each fortnight they would give him a lump sum, a stake from which he could build a modest empire (the trace of Jewish blood on his mother's side?) he would be set to live the ordered urbane life he craved.

No, he had to admit he was not feeling ill enough to merit a call to the doctor. He had been looking forward to a weekend away from it all. Couldn't she understand that the burden of anxiety was just as great for him and that he needed an admittedly undeserved break? What was he supposed to do during the weekend? No employers would be waiting with bated breath for his offers (pleadings more like) to work for them. She would be visiting her parents anyway, with the consensual proviso that he would not accompany her. The children were staying with his in-laws and though he wanted to see them he knew they sensed his feelings of guilt and inadequacy; they hardly could not, given the constant haranguing meted out by their mother.

His last visit to the 'Borgia' household, had surpassed all previous fraught encounters. Not in that there was family strife (he might have managed that) or open warfare and hatred (that was to come later) not the derisive ridicule from his eleven-year-old brother-in-law, but the studied indifference, surpassing contempt as it did, of his father-in-law.

He remembered the wedding day. The fulcrum. Till then the old man had kept schtum. It is not always easy to get a daughter off your hands, but it is especially desirable if you enjoy being cosseted by a none too brilliant wife and wish to lead a quiet life. There had not been a great surge of interest or clamour amongst young men for his daughter's hand in marriage. She was clever, not unattractive or totally forbidding; just a little cool and a lot too exact. The day had arrived, and he could relax his careful restraint "Where's this bridegroom?" he had asked, with a shade more irritation than warmth.

Light relief had needs been made of the shout and race along the railway platform. "Hold the train. Mister Strampet! Frederik Strampet!" Frederik had forgotten the ring. The chase, Strampet senior's only and near-fatal half-marathon easily trumped the news that the bride and groom's parents had not previously met and that the best man had been informed just that very day that he qualified as 'best' (God help the others) or indeed that there was a wedding in the offing.

Maybe that is when the rot set in. Or maybe it

started earlier; much much earlier. Maybe it started when Adam, though presumably possessed of all his faculties failed to ask his maker, why? Why must we not eat the fruit of the tree of knowledge? Should he not have said politely, "Hey dad, why, having given us understanding enough to receive your message not to eat of that particular tree (it looks much like all the others and if it is there, sooner or later we will surely touch it) may we not be given a reason why not? It would greatly help with our 'motivation' (which could become a big buzz-word one day) and go some way to reassure us regarding your fitness as a single parent."

It could be that Eve asked. Maybe she knew all the time. They say the more improbable the story the better it is believed and there is not much less likely than a talking snake. She was too smart to say it was a parrot.

In that far off time (not the Garden of Eden but the time in the garden suburbs of London of which we speak) there were two other main contenders for plaudits due, regarding the initiation and increase of the 'rot'. Now there are many other contenders; but more on that story later.

First there was the day, near the beginning, a day just like any other day before or since, all days of great moment, when a certain gatherer spake unto a certain hunter. She spoke thus.

"You are absolute rubbish with that spear, I could do better myself were I not carrying these triplets. Since you can't stick a pig with it, poke about in the dirt and push in as many of these seeds as you can, so that at least we can be sure something is growing here in a few months' time and I may get enough food to keep milk in my tits."

The hunter may have muttered, "Women! With their daft ideas," but he did as he was told, because not to, would have jeopardized his access to the said ~~tits~~ mammaries. After several Neolithic minutes of constructive criticism, the gatherer said, "For fuck sake give it here; they should have called you Wally not Fred. Now, you can be doing something useful while I am doing this, not waiting till – uh, that is a hard bit! - till –till-"

"Do stop tilling," said Fred "and tell me what you want me to do."

"You know the nanny goat that broke her leg and couldn't run away? Well I bound her leg, so she wouldn't fall over."

"You've not been using my garrotting sinews again have you?" moaned Fred.

"No, I used a piece of my old thong. Anyway, you

21

never garrotted anyone, none of you do; it's all show. Right to bear arms my elbow! Garrotting Club! Take out the enemy? They might take smegma out of their foreskins if they could find their willies beneath their fat guts! And when it comes to serious conflict, hide high up in the trees and drop fire onto shelters with women and children inside, is more what it amounts to. Anyway, I've tethered the nanny to a tree down by the river. I knew it was no use asking you to do it."

"So that's where it got to! I was looking forward to a big lump of goat-meat."

"I know you were, that is why I - Spirit of the Mountain, it's like talking to a tree trunk. Don't you see? We make sure she is well impregnated and then we can have milk and lots of baby goats. I want you to see that she has enough grass, but don't get too close to her."

Fred managed to look cheerful and puzzled at the same time.

"Well I got to get close don't I? I mean, impreg - impregating - you can't do that!"

"Not you, you great lummox, you omadhaun, you dummkopf, it has to be a billy goat, a wild billy goat. That is why she is tethered out there. God, it's not a husband I've got, it's an animal. Animal husbandry, that's what it is. And Fred, don't go telling everyone what we are doing. We may be prehistoric but we are not stupid, well some of us anyway; we will keep it to ourselves. If you meet anyone, just keep saying, 'This doth be and that doth be' and everything will seem normal."

Did Fred stay his mouth? Did he hell as like!

***

Meanwhile, Frederik had still to decide how ill he was. There was no doubting he was ill, but he knew the danger of succumbing to the social and economic pressures which attend the disabled and disadvantaged. His brief excursion into 'disabled employment' had taught him that; it was slave labour.

But wages are paid I hear you say; and slaves do not receive remuneration. True, but slaves have to be housed and fed (after a fashion) or exterminated, which all costs money; more money Frederik felt, than he was being paid.

"It's sheer exploitation," he had screamed, "you are exploiting my disability."

It had not gone down well with the highly regarded nation-wide organization in question, or in any other quarter; the truth seldom does.

But returning to possible reasons for Frederik's tribulations. Without doubt the industrial revolution was a cardinal cause in the dehumanising and debilitating process, which ultimately had dire effects on Frederik's health.

The Industrial Revolution took place in England and in every other developed country, especially Russia; both before and after she became the Soviet Union. Everything was invented again in each country, having first been invented a thousand years earlier in China. Its consequences were hard on the lungs, they were hard on the ears, they were hard on the uterus, the testicles, the environment and much, much more.

Machines became more important than people and so people tried to live like machines. Instead of living by the needs and sensibilities of the body, mind and soul, they were persuaded at first, then later compelled, to regulate their lives by the clock, the production process and the imperative of profit. It was what we succumbed to, so if Frederik was evaluated as a machine, indeed so judged himself, we should not complain or shrink from the incongruity of our declared policy, of not disposing of ineffective or obsolete machines, just because they happen to be human.

TARRY THE GRINDING

CHAPTER THREE

Having, as we do, a diminishing number of ancestors, at any given date the further back we go, we may imagine one such, of Frederik's. As a forebear of his, and almost certainly mine, and yours, we may name him Fred Rick, Goodman Rick as he was like to be called or, Mr. Frederik Richard Rick Esquire. He was perhaps an indifferent farmer. His father Frederik Archibald Rick, only slightly less indifferent and likewise his forbears stretching back (as all ancestries must) to our hunter Fred, who might have perished by the harsh course of nature, had it not been for the imaginative intervention of his lady wife, who by virtue of her singularity, was the best farmer of her day. The generation of Fred Rick was so far removed from her genius that the arrival of the industrial revolution, only just saved their bacon, in both the metaphoric and porcine sense. What for so long had been, both the means of and the bane of their toil torn existence, to wit the dirt beneath their feet, proved to be a mere cloak for a grimier substance below; black gold though it was. For some!

They were tenant farmers. Who owned the land? Who knew? Who cared? They cared; though little good it did them. So 'the rot' continued, though rot also brings about renewal.

Some ancestries which by dint of success in brutal conflict, fortune, or selective fawning, have become 'titled' (named) and choose to present themselves as 'Very Old Families,' even though families other than very old ones, do not exist. One such family, claiming they owned the land, said the coal deposits beneath the land, were also their property.

How can anyone 'own' land? (much less, the geology beneath it) other than the piece they live on; which portion is defined and observed by an instinctive code, which only the criminal or demented will violate. Should ownership extend through magma to the earth's core? perhaps beyond, to Australasia you might say; or upward into space; the moon, the planets and beyond. Such possibilities are no doubt being explored.

The Rick Clan might have fared worse; they broke from the land. One son became a moderately successful engineer, a daughter married a doctor and with the general drift, which became a surge that gravitated towards the towns and cities, they began the inhalation of impurities, which ultimately put paid to Frederik's lungs. Restricted inhalation also played a part, as citizens became reluctant to breath the polluted air of the great outdoors as well as the rank, fetid atmospheres of their overcrowded hastily constructed homes.

Frederik had much to say on the subject, but was unheard because he spoke mostly to himself and he cannot speak now because he is dead. I should know; I killed him!

To be fair I can't take all the credit, we all want action, change, progress, money; we all put the boot in somewhere. I killed him! You killed him! They killed him? Perhaps he killed himself. It is certain he went before his time, so someone must have done it. Euthanasia, suicide, murder?

Did one moment of neglect or indifference prove the proverbial straw to which the camel's back fell victim? Did the derisive guffaw from off-stage, as he ran from his loneliness to greet someone he loved, contribute? Did the demeanour of his friend which gave rise to the wound tinged response, "I am not here just for people's amusement," have a significantly adverse effect, or should the blame be laid at his capacity for conception of that thought?

***

If you want a divorce you first must be married and to marry you must promise, in effect, not to divorce. This creates a situation in which lawyers can guide two families through a labyrinth of grotesque possibilities for shaming each other. Did he make unnatural demands? Did she deny you your conjugal rights? Is he mad? Is she clinically sane? How drunk was she when she hit you? When did he start abusing the boy? These questions require the worst possible answers, which is where the lawyers score highly, because whatever is bad, they can make worse. The solution could be to make marriage illegal. Couples would still marry but would be less inclined to divorce.

Frederik's adversaries played the pornography card and the insanity card the mental cruelty card and for all we know, the Peter the Pie-man card. He was overwhelmed and in spite of a strange belated lust for Prudence (he became jealous of her gynaecologist) could not muster the energy to care very much. He wanted the love and respect of his children, some peace and what he despaired of ever receiving; relief from his agonizing struggle for breath.

The divorce would take a toll which, though not instantly 'soul destroying' or 'heart breaking' was nevertheless punishing; like a suspended capital punishment.

But of course, all that came later. Just now, Frederik had made it downstairs and it had not been easy either to decide upon, or to execute. Unable to find the shirt he wished to wear he had slowly and methodically donned his dressing gown. Halfway down the staircase he remembering he had not washed his nether regions, he hesitated, groaned and returned to the bathroom.

One of those bidet things he had seen in France would be useful. Mistakenly, he had thought it was for washing of feet. Soap, soap, where? Ah yes under the face flannel; better not use that. Can't wash it properly without easing back the foreskin, can be tricky either way, turgid or flaccid; not much chance of flaccid with this soap. Funny how it does exactly what it pleases, almost like a separate life, suppose that's why they call it 'the other.' I wonder if that dame is out there in the garden. She is probably at college or work. What is it about her? Even after all this time she can still - transfix - never even spoken to her but she knows — she must know; I can tell when we pass in the street. Never looks; it is as if she despises me. Enjoys my adoration though; oh yes. If I open the window just half an inch I can see if - my god, she's there. What a stroke of luck. No not luck. It is surely meant to be. Please God make her stay there, for pity sake don't go back inside now - no I'm sure she knows I'm looking at her - seeing - seeing - never seen her smile - she just moves - is that it? The way she moves? couldn't - can't stop now. Jesus Christ how beautiful - beautiful - beautiful - she - she - is.

***

At school he had incurred the detestation of the headmaster by his capacity for spending a whole lesson apparently diligently at work, producing nothing but a page covered in finger-marks, erasures and smudges. His hands were clammy; cold clammy, his saliva foamy, his speech muttered into his chin, ham-fisted and ill-footed at sport, his handicraft was catastrophically worse. He smelled vaguely like tomato soup and was popular with neither pupils nor staff. He failed his exams, not through lack of ability but because he detested the school and almost everyone in it.

Incredibly, he was pronounced fit to serve King and Country when the time came and was conscripted into the armed forces, who are notoriously reluctant to let go of;

31

even those they do not want. Interested parties may note that bed-wetting is one sure-fire option for 'working your ticket;' a point either unknown or passed over as being unhelpful to the plot, by the writers of the television series MASH. A drill sergeant can very easily detect a 'bod' trying to work his ticket, even though he cannot see that by listing the skives he 'knows you are up to,' he is providing a useful guide for the uninitiated.

Frederik proved their undoing. They sensed he was no use to them but abhorring the thought of anyone getting away with it, they tried to fit him to the mould. They failed.

Having been awarded punishment for some minor transgression, Frederik was given the summary task of cleaning the corporal's rifle. The NCO sat watching with fascination as Frederik fumbled and foamed his way through a ritual of obsessive procedures, which culminated with the four by two firmly stuck up the barrel. The corporal passed from red-faced fury to pale concern, completed the task himself and with weary resignation said, "I don't know Strampet, you worry me."

Frederik was eventually discharged on medical grounds, despite having satisfied the original panel of medical men that he was fit to serve. All such panels include a doctor (psychiatrist?) who deliberately treats the recruits (their patients let it be noted) like dirt. This presumably, is in order to ascertain whether or not they will break down in tears. That Frederik survived this ordeal is no surprise, as whatever his other deficiencies, he did not lack spunk. He also managed to survive the hell of initial training; though only just. What is a 'breeze' for some is purgatory for others. There are snide army tricks to contend with, such as the contriving of a hero at the top (the tallest or thickest) and a scapegoat at the bottom, (most sensitive or inadequate) and the accepted credo that if your gear is filched, you nick someone else's. For Frederik and his Flight, there was a lecherous Corporal's 'Reith Lecture' style account of his latest sex exploits, on the parade ground in pouring rain; standing to attention in tribute perhaps, to the N.C.O.'s discernibly erect penis. Is this part of the package? Who knows for sure? You certainly would not enquire of the Padre, who suggested to the twice-dampened recruits, that at this new phase of their lives, they might suitably join the church; and that, if they did not express that interest, he in turn, would not be interested in them.

Frederik was halfway through a technical course when the armed forces decided not to risk having to pay him a disability pension.

"Are you there, Frederik? I'm back. Your father has gone to the doctor's he should have gone yesterday; I told him, but he wouldn't go. Have you had a cup of coffee? I'll make coffee. You had better hurry if you are going out. There won't be time to drink it if you don't hurry."

Frederik was seated in the best easy chair, still in his dressing gown. "Hadn't you better get dressed if you are going out. Oh, you made coffee. You don't look well. I'll make you a fresh cup."

"I couldn't find my blue shirt."

"The light blue one? I washed it."

"I had only worn it once"

"I can iron it while the kettle is boiling. Couldn't you have worn another shirt? I ironed three of yours yesterday and two of your fathers."

"I told you, you only need to iron the collars and cuffs."

"Oh, I don't like half doing things. Your shoes don't look very clean. I 'll clean them for you while you drink your coffee; you want to make a good impression even though it's only the Labour Exchange. Have you had toast? I can get you those biscuits, the wholemeal ones; you need something. Are you sure you are well enough to go? You'll need to hurry if you are going. Your father should be back soon. What would you like for lunch?"

A cuckoo chick does not ask the surrogate parent not to fuss. Fussing is its due. Without fussing it would perish. But Frederik's was a natural parent and murderous; killing him as she was, with kindness.

Frederik's mother had been (and to his father) was still pretty. She was comfortably upholstered and calmly cheerful, which characteristics shared by Gudrun as they were, was perhaps why he was attracted to her. Also, the fact that he was attracted to any presentable female, and that Gudrun proved available, to the point of seducing him. Perhaps she was determined to get even with Prudence. Perhaps in Frederik, Gudrun discerned a sensitive and deserving heart.

Gudrun was almost fat but not mumsy. Prudence was lean and textbook mumsy. Between the two Frederik didn't stand a chance. They had a game to play and he didn't know the rules, because he didn't know the game. For Prudence it ceased to be a game when she failed to maintain supremacy. The peccadillo would have meant less if she'd had more self-assurance and talent in matters of the heart and the hips.

Frederik's driving ability was a prime target for

criticism from his wife even though it was something he did well; except when she criticized. Gudrun by contrast, was a passenger from heaven. She made light of a near miss that was only thirty per-cent his fault. "You took your eyes off the road didn't you, you naughty boy."

Frederik coughed lightly, "I was just checking we have enough petrol."

"I think you were looking at my legs."

Frederik coughed again, looked at the petrol gauge, then at her legs.

"Oh for goodness sake; pull over into that lay-by and I'll give you a proper look."

There was a rail strike in progress, or a go slow, work to rule or a 'wild cat' strike. Gudrun had been their guest on a weekend visit. Prudence was now at work.

"He could certainly go slow, but he couldn't work to rule, he is never in a job long enough to get acquainted with the rules and just because Gudrun is here doesn't mean you don't have to vacuum the carpet, if you can call it a carpet. We will be in the garden looking at the flowers we haven't got because we can't afford bedding plants. You can give Gudrun a lift home tomorrow morning, at least it will get you out of bed." This and more unrestrained commentary, had not enhanced the social quality of the weekend, or bolstered Frederik's tattered self-esteem.

The car's sudden swerve and halt seemed to match the atmosphere of excited anticipation. Gudrun hitched her skirt up to her waist. "There. I know they are a little bit chubby, but they are better than Pru's. The skin is nice and silky; feel."

Frederik felt. Red of face, his lungs filling with air, his heart with wonder and gratitude, he graced her with his best feature; a quite appealing smile. She rearranged her dress. "You poor bugger. Nobody deserves that. Prudence has always been rather brittle, but she surpassed herself this weekend. You shouldn't put up with it; assert your manhood." What Frederik did next, induced a reaction, something between a giggle and a gasp, which only certain women can achieve with charm. "I don't mean here and now, - no -no - Freddie! Wait till we get to my place." He managed a feeble "What then?" wondering obliquely if he should stop to buy condoms. She kissed his cheek. "We shall have to wait and see, shan't we." Gudrun contributed to a stay of execution, but ultimately, she could not save his life.

What does it feel like to be on death row? Well, we make the best of things don't we.

Contrary to his instinct and inclination, Frederik submitted himself to higher authority and power; namely, medical science. At other times and in other places, such powers might have been the Church, the Shaman or the Seer. They tested him for every allergy known to man and medicine. They scratched, scraped, injected and directed him. He digested, ingested, was pummelled, probed and prodded. Some of the more theatrical manipulations had short-term beneficial effects and the Class 'A' type injections produced reactions which, under less controlled conditions might have earned him three months in the slammer, but the supreme unworldly judges said "No." Frederik's mental and physical shortcomings would not be mended.

What moves those greater forces; or fails to move them more often, and who are they anyway. Does indifference play a part? Does spite? We must fervently hope not. Moreover, if as in Frederik's case, we do not believe in such greater unearthly powers, we must be content to negotiate with earthly forces, which besides medical and scientific, will include economic, social, political and sundry others and have, already made their mark. So, who to appeal to, or blame?

In a Hollywood movie we know it is the State

Governor, whom we perceive to be a reactionary crook, but in real life (what is 'real' about it?) we have a problem. We have a host of problems, for starters whether to face them or not. Whether to take arms against, or tranquilisers because of them. You can pop along to your over-worked, under-resourced GP and he will relieve his own stress, by taking the line of least resistance and give you choice of colour in tablets recommended (prescribe these or else) by a drug company which has judiciously suppressed the results of any tests which high-lighted their side effects. "No, they are not addictive but don't come off them suddenly." Why come off them at all you may think, if they are as good as he says they are. It is cheaper than getting drunk and you can impress your friends.

"He," or increasingly, "She - has put me on 'Scrotamtomiosin' they are green."

"I haven't heard of them."

"No you won't have; they are new. They are from America."

Is there any other profession, trade or occupation where it is not incumbent upon the supplicant to demonstrate some ability in the field in which they hope to qualify and practise?

"Not a bad little bit of joinery is that. I think I might

reckon to take you on."

"I caught the tail end of your speech to the 'Young Maniacs' last Thursday. I was impressed by the way you hurled most of the missiles back at them. Welcome to the 'Seriously Deranged & Dangerously Infantile Party.'

"I come not to seize a Caesar - sorry can I start again?"

And so forth, but not, "That's right, a concert violinist. I thought I might pick it up as we went along."

However, enquire of a prospective medical student if they have ever cured anyone of anything and you will be set for a good laugh.

"Do me a favour! Sick people put me about. I got top 'A' levels in maths and science though."

No problem then, with keeping tally of the patients who drop dead.

"I don't think I've ever come across anyone really depressingly ill. No wait, I had a hamster once; didn't look at all well. What did I do? Returned it to the pet shop and got my money back, what do you think."

Yet still we continue to have complete and absolute faith in modern medicine, despite its manifold mishaps and catastrophic failings. We should also bear in mind that it is only modern today; tomorrow it will be practice of the past. We meet our doctor's jaundiced eye, hoping he is not one of the admittedly few practitioners, who is reducing his workload by, initially discreet, but increasingly blatant, murder; in the suppressed hope apparently, that disclosure of his method of 'treatment' will finally relieve him of his awesome responsibility.

"Can't you see I am in a worse state than you are, you idiot." he must be thinking, "I am not God almighty; I never said I was. Granted my remuneration is reasonable, but you have to take account of the frequent and far-flung vacations I need to take to bolster my aura of superiority, which you insist I maintain and to put as great a distance between myself and you as is earthly possible!"

A common communal blind spot (one of how many?) facilitates a denial of the fact that images of the gregarious G.P., quaffing a friendly pint with his patients in the local hostelry, is confined to television soap operas.

We choose not to notice that as each scourge of humanity is eliminated, a new one emerges, or a peripheral malady is on the increase.

Though debate about the desirability of designer babies affords a relatively anodyne field for discussion, choice of ailment or infirmity, may be more controversial; but are things not moving in that direction?

For someone who uses an electric (pedestrian shunting) buggy and a stair lift in preference to walking, bipedal locomotion, therefore legs, may become superfluous to requirement. Anyone with an aversion to the stresses of emotional involvement with creatures of their own kind, with a leaning towards narcotic substitution, might like to have that part of the brain (identifiable these days) which copes with such matters, removed. Artificial insemination has been with us long enough now to be an attractive alternative to the exertion and viscositous nature of procreation by the traditional method.

So may have run Frederik's thoughts, or may not have: will we ever know? Could cranial archaeology become low-cost television programming in the future? Whatever brain activity took place in Frederik Strampet's head (and something surely did that wet summer morning) must have left traces - chemical - electrical - micro-molecular, which may at some time be deciphered, interpreted and ultimately presented; with whatever concessions to commercial viability are deemed necessary. Fetched too far-flung from afar? Consider what early twentieth century comprehension regarding the science of D.N.A. would have been, and think again.

What did he want for lunch? Frederik considered. He did not so much think, as picture. He pictured every food, every dish, every menu, each delicacy that ever was, and he wanted them all. It was not so much greed as need for release from greed. It was a pitiful reach for oblivion. He yearned to be absorbed in the process of eating, to be relieved from his anguish and stress. What would it be like to live as a ruminant; a cow in a field, constantly feeding? To fulfil an unnatural imperative to eat full-time; blotting out all troubles, consciousness, and worldly affairs.

"While you are thinking, I can be getting on with ours. Your father will have some kidneys. I don't want much. Are you still a vegetarian? Prudence said she found it too much trouble. There is plenty of salad."

"Oh sorry, I was just - yes - ccchhh - in theory yes. Salad."

Salad was all very well, but you needed to eat so much of it and it did not possess you in the way that starchy foods did. He remembered with regret, an avid attack he had launched on a salad, which had resulted in him chipping a front tooth when he bit on his fork in his frenzied striving for gastronomic nirvana.

Should he allow himself a little indulgence today? He had over-eaten the previous evening, his mother having as usual, prepared and presented him with too much food. Once he started, he seemed unable to stop eating; because *she* never stopped talking. Did not stop? Would not? Could not? Perhaps her compulsion was as strong as his. He had heard about battered husbands and he envied them. Anything would be better than her relentless, indefatigable tongue. Worse still was, that he knew she was right.

"And another thing. I have never seen anyone eat so much except perhaps that so-called friend of yours. The two of you should get together, you could easily break the world record for gluttony; at least that would be some achievement; and the state of you both. You certainly lowered the tone of Eastbourne; I can never go there again. You seem to delight in looking scruffy and untidy when he's around, you need to grow up, both of you. Not that I care what he does, but you will certainly have to change your ways."

She continued with considerable force and invention, but he was able to detach himself from the onslaught to some extent and as long as he looked meek enough, she didn't notice.

That time he had sunk to the ground in the middle of the entrance to a builders yard in Swansea. Was that not 'grown-up' enough? Was that not a mature Herculean effort, not to give in to his uncalled-for debility? That location was not a professional invalid's choice of a place to rest was it? There was proximate sand, but no beach.

As a holiday adventure journey, it should never have been undertaken. The time of year, the climate erratic in everything except the certainty of high pollen counts. Closer to a near death than a life enhancing experience. The 'recorder' in attendance, at times needing to be a burdened beast of both their rucksacks, lending him substance: he at the time, almost a shadow.

One night there was not an uncultivated square foot of land to be found and the straw-stack which was to become their ultimate flop, was suspected by night smell of being, and was proven by daylight to be, a dung heap.

There was light and dark relief. "You can't camp yer. There's no camping yer see. There's a perfectly good campsite down the road; you can go there. You come down yer, you don't want no trouble see."

Hardly ever was a truer word spoken and the unspoken,' We know mate, but we don't like campsites and having spent one night here under your very nose we are moving on anyway,' was also true. No sense in trying to explain that it was not just a matter of choice, but also of principle and a philosophy of being a tight-wad and 'different.'

Others were more accommodating. "I was just a'thinkin,' that piece o' meadow down by the barn." A thirteen-year-old exercising generous authority (good lad, don't let the bastards get to you, but they probably did) "you could camp there - if it's only for one night"

Frederik should have died then, but he didn't. Or maybe he should have died later, alone on a beach; but he lived on. Just.

***

Last evening had not been the best time to broach the matter; he knew that, but he also knew that no time was a good time. Good times to intimate the possibility of a weekend camping trip did not exist. First, she didn't hear, then she heard but did not believe she heard, then she didn't believe what she heard.

"Are you completely out of your mind? Who has been at work all week? Who got soaking wet running for the bus because the car has fallen to pieces. I'm going to my parents rather than impose too much on yours! I'm the one who should be having a weekend break."

"You could come with us." He knew she wouldn't.

The idea was absurd. Had she agreed to go, it would have been far worse than not going at all.

Her astonished gasp almost initiated tears.

"I have already been humiliated, do not insult me as well. Are you seriously suggesting I traipse around the country side like a gypsy, begging for lifts and a place to stay." Frederik could only grin sheepishly. "You are impossible." she shouted and then, nearing hysteria. "Perhaps you would like me to walk the streets! Is that what you want?"

For a moment the thought appealed to him. It might warm and soften her (if she didn't, she wouldn't earn much) and could hardly further cool or harden her tungsten conformation. But in the same moment he knew it was not a fair assessment of her nature. There was another side of her, or had been. She must really have believed she could change him. Had she loved him as he was, or as she thought she could shape and modify him? Was she capable of love, which could detach itself from judgment?

She was a middle child and as so often, not the hoped-for male heir. Until choice of sex in offspring becomes a reality (as it will become, legally or otherwise) many middle and third upwards girls, will continue to live as ghosts.

Or, perhaps. "We appreciate you are next in the queue, but your must needs wait until your prospective parents are bored by having sons."

Maybe it wasn't that. Maybe it was just that, as a run of the mill looker, no more and perhaps a bit less, she was certainly not an earth-shattering drop-dead beauty; which is what all women want to be; and who has the heart to blame them?

Rather as with the killer instinct in the male (the really strong man being one who, though he could, has no wish to kill) so with female beauty, the few so passing lovely they could destroy the world, do not so do, because by being beautiful they are also good. And those, not quite of that sacred conformation, are not able to change the world. And at last beauty has gone.

Who's got the beauty? It could be in the eye of the beholder where no one else can get at it. It is not always with those who think they have it, not with those who believe they can buy it, and it is certainly not with the publicity freaks, who seek to steal it.

Prudence was capable of tenderness, but Frederik had given new meaning to phrases like 'unbelievably exasperating' and 'monumentally inept.' She was at the end of her tether and her tongue was over-active with speech and unused where it would have eased their suffering.

"No I just thought -" "Well don't think," she snapped.

"But we have made arrangements, I can't just say I'm not going!"

"Oh can't you? Well I can!" And she did.

***

There was no escaping the situation. He would have to sign on.

"I'll have a cheese salad." This to his mother as he opened the front door.

"You'll need more than that. Shall I scramble some eggs as well? There is still some meatless savoury roll, you could have some of that."

"Yes alright, I've got to go."

"What time will you be -"

Frederik closed the front door. Getting himself ready had taken longer than it should have. He was late. Was it worth seeing if the car would start? It was standing on the short drive next to his two other vehicles (one on the lawn, the other over a flower bed) neither had survived protracted decline. Standing, rather than parked, as the latter suggests a possible resumption of mobility. He had not forgotten to pick up the keys (a good omen) and as he inserted the key of the broken door lock into the ignition, his irritation was mollified (as he changed keys) by a pleasant glow of expectation. The weather was warmer and the battery might have had time to recuperate. Seated purposefully in the vehicle's sagging seat, Frederik attempted to activate the engine. His efforts failed and its stubborn refusal to function appeared to him as a rebuke. He had subjected it to the indignity of apprehension by the Police, for displaying false road tax authorisation. He had substituted it's out of date tax disk with another, from one of the immobile vehicles. Attending at court in the confident belief that his idea of justice would prevail, he explained to the magistrate that the two cars were exactly the same make, year and model. "The other car was off the road," he explained, "there was no possibility of it being driven, it was irrevocably unserviceable, immobile and dysfunctional." But it was all to no avail.

"And do you know what? The bastard even congratulated the copper on his diligence." He informed the 'intimate;' quietly, lest others might hear, but not have cognisance of the depth of his disgust.

Give it another chance. After a short prayer to his non-existent God, he turned the key and pressed the starter again.

It tried. Credit should be given for effort. 'That is better,' Frederik thought, 'last time there was nothing.'

Given that this result amounted to complete failure as far as getting him into town was concerned, Frederik's satisfaction was inordinate; but such was his nature. He lived in another world.

Just one more try he thought. This time the car only managed an exhausted swish and click. Almost in unison, prolapsed vehicle and would-be driver pronounced, "Shit." He had to smile.

It would have to be the bus. Damn; he hoped he hadn't missed it. No, just right; there it was approaching the request stop. Cross the road quite casually; no need to break into a run, as would a schoolboy or a nervous old lady. Not quite at the stop, he raised his hand in the manner of an unshaven Hollywood 'B' movie actor. The public service vehicle did not stop.

'The bastard! He's pretended he hasn't seen me. I bet it was that idiot I had words with the other day.'

He had enquired what time the last bus left the station. "Do you mean the railway station or the bus depot?" "The railway station of course, if I had meant bus depot -" "A lot of people say bus station when they mean bus depot." "Well I - - don't." Frederik was having breathing difficulty. "Could you give me the information please?" "Would that be Weekdays or Sundays?" "Saturday actually." "That's Weekdays then innit." "Well no. In point of fact Saturday is not a Weekday." "I don't do Satdys." Frederik gulped into his wheeze. "If you could just tell me -" "I just told you, I don't do Satdys." "Yes I understand, but surely that does not preclude you from knowing the time of the last bus." "Oh my gawd, 'ow many times! I told you, I don't do Satdys. This ain't no bleedin' Twenty Questions. Best thing for you squire is, buy yourself a timetable."

What had the country come to. It was those goddam Socialists! Nobody knew their places anymore. Frederik had undergone a swing from left to right; he of all people, who was about as entrepreneurial, as a wounded hedgehog. It had not been the classic swing, coinciding as it should have, with acquisition and increased prosperity. Rather than acquiring horses (he had read Hemmingway so was acquainted with the classic process) he had lost the use of two and a half motorcars and possession of a roof over his head.

The dalliance with his eccentric uncle's addled idealism had borne meagre fruit. His father's influence had prevailed in spite of his uncle's more sympathetic nature. Respectability came above everything else; even comfort. His parents' house was subsiding into a semi bog, but was in a better area than where they would have had to move.

Nothing for it but to walk; it started raining again. That was it! 'Today I ain't takin' no crap from no one.' That's the way they talk, our coloured brethren. For some queer reason, his thoughts turned to their relaxed easy seeming attitude to life, with its parallel world of intensity and to him, smouldering menace. He pictured Jimmie Hendrix with a disturbing blend of fascination and repugnance. How dare he look like that! No one had a right to look like that; to be like that. Yet he was. If it was so out of Frederik's world, so beyond his ken, why was he so taken and moved. He thought of that big black, drunk West Indian in the NAAFI who had unzipped and began stroking his huge pink-tipped member. "Wan'a woman. Wan'a woman" he had said; direct, to the point and to hell with the consequences.

At the labour office, the anticipated encounter did not happen. She was not there; *he* was not there. It was someone different; someone he knew but who he desperately tried to pretend he did not recognise. Sensing mutual embarrassment, they both avoided eye contact. "Sign here please," the youth said. Frederik hesitated. His signature would confirm his identity and validate their shared school past, with its farcical, petty and brutal episodes. Which is more shaming, to be unemployed or to be employed?

As he left the building he could see his bus approaching. His determination not to miss it unleashed a surge of adrenaline, which nearly burst his heart. He sprinted along the wet pavement, arms flaying frantically, and he hurled himself into the road.

The driver spoke. "What's your game? This is not a suicide facility! It's not even a request stop. It's an obligatory."

"I merely wished to," gasped Frederik, "make sure you saw -" gasping transcended words and he settled for silence and sorely restricted breathing. The conductor looked to the sky. "I thought it was Nijinsky practising his pirouettes."

Oh, this one's a smart-arse. If anything is worse than an ignoramus, it is a smart-arse. Probably a party official just returned from a Trade Union University Scholarship, filling in time till he could seize dictatorship at the top.

Had Frederik been able to think, he could not have spoken, and he could barely see through the newsprint-picture haze which had descended upon his vision. Had he spoken he might have said "I am sorry, I am ill-equipped to cope with life's stresses. Please acknowledge the variations in capability, of individual specimens of humankind. Make allowance for personal idiosyncrasies, the inadequacies of the enfeebled; cherish the otherness of the odd-ball." But of course, he didn't.

CHAPTER FOUR

Mealtime in the Strampet household verged on the ceremonial. Everything Mr. Strampet senior did, tended towards ceremony. His acts of procreation had probably been formalized in all but the final flourish. As Frederik sat down, his father slid his serviette from its ring. "Your mother and I have been waiting nearly half an hour."

"You should have started without me; I might have been delayed even longer."

Mr. Strampet tested the kidney before making his reply. "Meal-time is meal-time," he said.

Mrs. Strampet did not breathe; at least not perceptibly. She took delicate little gasps of air occasionally, which seemed to fulfil her respiratory needs quite adequately. Mr. Strampet's breathing would have been stentorian except that it sounded pained and grudging; centred in his head. Frederik's breathing centred in a small space deep inside his chest, his mother's centred at her heart. They rendered a strange trio; treble recorder, un-restored sackbut and grievously damaged harmonium.

"When are you going to do something about those vehicles in the garden? They can't stay there till they rot."

"I'm hoping to get at least one of them back on the road as soon as possible."

"But you've been saying that for the past four months."

"There is a certain difficulty in obtaining particular parts. Those cars are not actually in anyone's way there are they."

"They are on top of my dahlias. This is not a scrap yard. We have to live here amongst neighbours who expect certain standards to maintain."

Frederik searched his stock of get-outs (all, to him, quite genuine) accumulated during half a lifetime of over-use. His mother affected his rescue, if not his vindication.

"Prudence said her father considered there is not a hope in hell - no real chance of making them road-worthy; and he's an engineer."

"Prudence's father - her father, is not a mechanic first of all and he has never even seen two of those cars and anyway he doesn't like the idea of me owning three cars."

"He might be quite taken with the idea of you owning one that would go somewhere though, might he not?" Mr. Strampet had a lumbering sarcasm at his command.

"That car is perfectly - there is nothing wrong with that car. At the moment it won't start, that's all."

"Prudence said her foot went through the floor." Treble recorder.

"She was exaggerating; it was only her toe; it needs welding. Not her toe of course."

"Oh Frederik, we didn't think you meant her toe. Poor Prudence, she doesn't need her toe welding." Hysteria tinged, ersatz merry and superfluous but kindly meant recorder solo.

"It is no laughing matter; the bloody thing is a death trap."

"Please Horace; not at table."

Frederik was not a silent eater at the best of times (are any of us except those who oppress us with their 'perfect' manners) and this was not the best of times. As he crunched his decreasingly tempting salad, the sound reverberating through his skull, appeared to fill the dining room; or would have, had they been lunching in the dining room.

'The dining room is presently out of commission due to the stench of cat piss.' I could say more but they are eating.

Cats did not like the male Strampets. They didn't know why; they just didn't like them; it was something about the way they look at you. They adored Mrs. Strampet, but then most *people* did, though they did not always realize it; she was not a demanding woman. And what a precious rarity that is.

The meal continued for the most part in verbal, if not masticatory silence. The slight sounds with their accompanying and unnecessary apologies, which would be unremarkable in the gentle hubbub of fork on plate, the odd 'Ho hum' of the mythical 'average' family repast, took on a guilt-laden quality with the Strampets.

Luncheon terminated, Frederik put one plate on top of another, then took it off again. He thoughtfully moved a teacup, then its saucer partner; then another cup. His father had taken his own utensils to the kitchen, so to speak (having eaten there, they were already in the kitchen) and half stalked, half staggered into the lounge with yesterday's edition of the 'Times.'

"Shall I help you clear away?" Frederik asked.

"No thank you Frederik I can manage. You had better be getting on with writing those applications. Prudence will be asking what you have done."

Should he write the letters upstairs or downstairs. Downstairs his father's accusatory presence and heavy breathing would be distracting, upstairs his mother's tidying and careful non-intervention might be worse. Few people's presence afforded him the ease of being which we all yearn for (he took the so-called friend for granted) but there had been Barco who had loved him, and whom he had loved. Frederik had enrolled at a minor London college where he had managed to coalesce enough of his tattered education to gain a certificate of general academic competence. The old tutor had taken a shine to Frederik from the start. Too circumspect (and perhaps too decrepit) to go beyond furtive caresses and gropes, he had spoken much of Socrates and others. The unpronounceability of his real name and his unknown origin did not matter. He was acknowledged by the students as a true and inspired teacher who had never wished to be anything else; but he was known for not caring he was unknown, and in the world of ambitious advancement there is no greater sin.

Frederik suffered the snide remarks and sidelong smirks (some envious) of the male students with little regret. As for the girls, somehow it didn't seem to matter very much. His head and heart were filled with Barco who was the first and perhaps the last person (besides his mother) who did not treat him like, and crucially, make him feel like, an absolute idiot.

Making a space at her dressing table (better remember where to replace her limited makeup items) he settled down to begin. 'That's interesting. Never really examined my profile in this light before; almost classic. Pity about the broken cartilage in the nose, never knew till that doctor told me; wonder when it happened, got punched so many times in junior school. Never cried though. Not really bullied either; just considered a prat.'

All the courses he had attended. All the jobs he had had. Had, was right! "You've had it mate; you're driving on your luck. One more bump and you're out on your arse." That, the precursor to his exit from a government driving job.

"Do you know what they had me doing?" (this to the confessor) "They had me working as a chain man. I was given that job as a qualified surveyor!"

And there was the fantastic notion of working both day and night shifts as a railway porter, (in the days when there were such) at the same station would you believe, together with the even 'brighter' idea that he wouldn't need to sleep! "Surely someone will notice you are working both shifts?" The 'confessor' could not believe what he was hearing. "Well no, because it will be different personnel." For a time, no one noticed. No one had conception of anything so weird.

"Oi mate, this ain't no kip."

"Wake up sleeping beauty - - can't shift him."

"Is he pissed?"

"Can't smell nuffink."

"I fink 'e's dead."

" 'E's breavin' - can't be dead."

"Well he ain't sleeping on my shift, give him a whack!"

"I've whacked 'im free times. What's 'is name?"

"Strampet. No can't be. Strampet works days, unless there's another Strampet."

"Are you sure? Can't be no one else wiv a name like that."

"Let's see. Narr, I don't believe it - I don't fucking believe it! The cunt's only got hisself down on both shifts!"

The only portering Frederik subsequently did, was carrying his cards away when he regained consciousness twenty-six hours later.

He had to admit the idea had not worked out as intended, especially as he was not paid the triple time he had claimed in an elaborate overtime scheme he had dreamt up with hours overlapping the two shifts. So, the elusive 'stake' which was to set him up for life, had not materialized.

If he could just get a start in business, he would be set on the course he craved. He had no idea what kind of business, no business experience or expertise, but he was enamoured of the magic word 'business' which meant money; lots of money and an easy life.

Think not however, that that was his only dream. He had many others.

If Paul Gauguin and Vincent Van Gogh could do it, surely he also could! Having gained admission to a minor Art School in Oxford he set to, with brush, paint and pallet. He quickly noticed that what was needed to fit into the pattern of student life at Oxford. "It doesn't matter how old and worn your clothes may be, so long as," he informed the 'observer,' "they were once of the very highest quality." He was perceptive enough in such matters but was unable to follow through with the poise necessary for the social success he craved and was sure he deserved.

Education establishments need students and cannot be so exacting in standards of ability as to compromise the acquiring of fees. He produced a small number of paintings, which were puzzling in as much as it was impossible to believe he could not see how bad they were.

Evidencing urgently needed but fragile self-belief, he said, "See how I have exaggerated everything. Can you see how I have taken the lapel of the jacket right over the shoulder, to express the horror of the future."

Recipient of aesthetic analysis replied. "No. What it expresses to me is that you have conflicting desires, both to wear and not to wear a zoot suit."

He had basked in the glory of Oxford, though he remained untouched and unnoticed and might have experienced a full sense of 'arrival' (he was a career student) had it not been for a disastrous visit by the 'incubus' who punctured his bladder of respectability.

"That landlady was never the same with me after your visit. I tried to explain that you were putting on an act but the more I tried the less she believed me. Not everyone in Oxford is sympathetic to Socratic thinking."

How long do thoughts, ideas and reminiscences take to pass through our mind? Do they indeed pass through? If they 'pass through' they must come from and proceed on to, somewhere else. Could they emanate from another brain (we believe in radio waves) or be capable of entering and influencing other thought processes? That there is a discernible difference between the 'feel' of things living and of the lifeless is undeniable, so may not traces of thought processes (chemical, electrical?) leach from one to another? Do they surface willy-nilly, because mostly they are with us, or present themselves whenever they feel like it; or refuse to present themselves, if other - other what? - dreams, urges, forces, forbid them?

Whatever Frederik's thoughts were, or from whence they came that day, they had occupied thirty seconds (or perhaps thirty minutes) more before he realized he was not in possession of a pen. Writing paper he had, dictionary he had, pen he had not.

She must have a pen in here somewhere - pen - pen - no - panties; that frilly see-through pair he had given her. Not even in her underwear drawer; cast amongst the bits and bobs.

"If you think I am going to wear those, you are very much mistaken. I would catch my death of cold for one thing."

"They are not actually to wear as such - just for - well you know."

He had presented his foolish grin, which she had long ceased to find attractive.

"You amaze me, you really do amaze me. Did you seriously think I would parade around in those things to further stimulate your over-active libido? How much did they cost? - wasting money we can ill-afford - they set the prices sky high in order to exploit fools like you."

"They weren't very expensive, I bought them at Marks and Spencers."

"Oh, so I'm only worth a cheap pair am I? Now you add insult to injury."

He had not purchased them at Marks and Spencer, as she would have seen, had she bothered to look properly. They had cost far too much. He had been taken for a ride! Could she not for once have put aside her scathing scruples and indulged herself and him for a short time?

That's what the girls in the park used to say. "Do you want a short time?" 'No! I would like a long time! A long lingering earth-shattering, world-shuddering long time! A dreaming, demented, youth-blinding long time.' But you had to settle for a short time.

Frederik fingered the soft silky fabric. What a waste. He wondered what it would feel like to wear them, they were so flimsy, ethereal, almost non-existent; in his hand no weight at all.

His father would be dozing, his mother — better put

a chair against the door just in case. He exchanged his slacks for the pretty panties and held up his shirt. 'That just looks ridiculous,' he thought. Framed in the full-length mirror, emphasis appeared to centre on his socks. Might as well do a proper job. He removed the socks and stripped down to his freckled pelt. Not bad, though the half-interested 'hampton' was somewhat out of place, especially as it was glancing to one side. It had an eye (it's one and only, obviously) on the door. And well it might, because just as Frederik was striking his second pose, the door rattled and spoke.

"Have you taken my pen? What the hell's going on! Frederik are you in there; what's wrong with this door!"

"No I'm not. I mean no, I haven't got your pen. I'm writing letters, I can't find my pen."

There was an expression of exasperated and indifferently suppressed blasphemy.

"I've got your pen, I want mine."

As Frederik made a grab for his shirt, something fell from the pocket onto the carpet; it was his father's pen. Abandoning hope of donning the shirt, he tried frantically to divest himself of the panties, stubbing his toe and nearly completing a forward double, with twist and pike. You can fall head over heels in love, you can lose your balance and take a tumble, but the fall, which Frederik executed, could only be properly described as 'arse over tit.'

"Whatever is going on - have you hurt yourself?"

Forcing open the door, Strampet senior entered the bedroom and was confronted by his son, naked and ashamed.

"I was changing," he said lamely. There had not been time to conceal the scanties under the bed covers, but the solution to his emergency, was in the word scanties. He had scrunched them into the palm of his hand.

"Why? - What?" Looking grey faced and glossy Mr. Strampet swayed slightly. Frederik stepped forward as if to support his father. His father swayed away. The mere prospect of the cardigan touching the naked flesh, was enough to affect several recovery.

"No, I am alright. It doesn't matter about the pen. Keep it!"

Left to himself, Frederik resumed his position at the dressing table. Having lived with embarrassment for a large part of his life, he was able to adapt quite quickly. 'I had better get on with this now, though that toe will be painful for a few days. And my elbow and ribs.' No point in dwelling on the matter it could have been worse. Socks and vest only; that is when a man looks really ridiculous.

Or, naked with a paunch. At least he had a flat gut.

'To womb it may concern.' Could send it like that for all the difference it would make. 'Dear Sir or Madam.' Only needs an 'a' and a 'c' and I could be shovelling tarmac in no time at all. Or capitalize 'C' and 'A' and I could usher ladies of lower income, into those popular stores, in a manner to which they would like to become accustomed. "Does Madam require the, cch cch, lingerie department?" Might make some good connections that way, but then again they would be mostly old boilers.

"Your father said you fell over. Did you fall over? How did you fall over?"

His mother had entered silently, causing him to jump out of his now fully clothed skin.

"Do these belong to Prudence, aren't they pretty, I've never seen her in those."

'Neither have I,' he though ruefully. He knew what his mother meant even if she did not. "Well they are certainly not mine. I just tripped that's all."

"You should be more careful; you might have hurt yourself."

I have only broken three ribs he thought; but was in no mood to receive his mother's sympathy.

"Will you need sandwiches tomorrow if you are

going away?"

"I'm not going away."

"There is some nice watercress to go with the cheese because you don't eat ham and hard boiled eggs are useful because you don't need to worry about breaking them, well you have to break them anyway don't you and we've plenty of wholemeal bread. You are not going away?"

"I am not going away."

"Well if you are not going away, you won't be needing sandwiches I suppose. Does Prudence know?"

"Yes, Prudence knows."

"Will it disturb you if I hoover the other bedrooms?"

"No, it will not disturb me."

"Alright then I'll hoover the other bedrooms and the landing. I can leave this room till tomorrow when you are away so as not to disturb you. Oh, of course you are not going away are you, I'm getting so forgetful."

She left, closing the door quietly and Frederik sighed as deeply as his inadequate lungs and bruised ribs would allow. He could have done without the distraction.

Why should not the least co-ordinated musculature, attempt excellence in a discipline requiring exceptional aptitude, skill and precision? Ask Frederik! He had splashed, belly-flopped and back-cricked his way through a regime of self-improvement which had moved a diving coach to remark, "Well at least you can't get any worse." He had forced his way backwards on the best ice skates money could buy, whilst being able to progress forward, in a manner to be described at best inelegant, at worst grotesque. He had danced on dainty feet which unfortunately were not his own. He had attempted to sing, in an apparent bid to prove his 'accomplice' correct, when he had asserted that Frederik was tone deaf; thus showing his ineptitude was not restricted to physical grace. But he had tried!

With Hedy Lamarr it was different; endeavour was unnecessary. Without effort or intent, he had fallen in love with Hedy Lamarr; or thought he had. In fact, he had been cajoled, brainwashed, indoctrinated, 'Hollywood mesmerised' into being — as was almost everyone of that time — in love with a shadow.

He would sit through two double cinema performances and emerge wrung-out with frustration and longing, his brain reiterating the information that she had once been filmed naked. Hedy Lamarr naked! He had read how her husband had tried to acquire every copy of the film. Did he wish to destroy them all? Jealously keep every copy for himself? Why take the trouble if he possessed the original thing. The words 'thing' and 'possess' should not sit easily when referring to human beings, but Hollywood had made those words, in such settings, seem appropriate. Frederik was 'possessed' in another sense; as perhaps also were the star's husband, the voyeur cameraman and a million fans, but simultaneously as they so 'possessed' Hedy Lamarr and were themselves 'possessed,' they were dispossessed of their own reality.

In those days, you smoked like the stars, you talked like, walked like and as far as possible, looked like the stars; if you didn't you were nothing. And they had to be Hollywood stars because there were no others. British Films you treated with the 'contempt they deserved' and that 'Cinema,' was being produced in other parts of the world never entered your ken. Hollywood had everything buttoned up; tight. You did not know and would not have cared that the British film industry, controlled as it was by American money was allowed only second-rate lighting, technical equipment and resources. You ignored, or were uninformed, that many Hollywood actors were British or if not, had to assume English sounding names. You did not notice that the scowling hero hammering the telephone and shouting "Operator! Operator!" had already cut himself off and that the wounded 'fall guy' might have survived, if they had not forced brandy down his throat.

You swaggered, leered, grinned or scowled your way through life, timorously not realizing that your opposing posers were as full of bunk as you were. It would have been easy to notice (perhaps was noticed but not acknowledged) that most of the better actors were pretty ghastly looking and that the beauteous and handsome were not so much bad actors, as not actors at all. But you dare not step out of line; or was it that you did not want to shatter your own illusions? You strutted your Hollywood fake personality. Frederik could ham it with the best and fail with the worst.

And so it was, that just as we were being regaled by images of physical perfection, never before presentable in such quantity, medical technology and procedure was busy rescuing the halt and the lame. The survival of pitifully premature and disastrously disadvantaged human offspring was made possible for those whose chance of attaining Hollywood standards of bodily desirability, was impossible. The idea that you could smoke, drink and accent-speak your way to Movie Star desirability, was insinuated into the human psyche, with a compelling effect, hitherto impossible.

Just as we reached the point where to doubt the theory of natural selection was to court scorn and ridicule, we set about reversing its purpose. Just when the industrial revolution was accelerating the process of eliminating all but the most robust of human specimens, medical science stepped up and put a spanner in the works. Those who were condemned by nature to infertility, were reinstated by science into the process of 'natural' selection. Did anyone think about it? Certainly the Nazi's did, though we prefer to use their solution as an excuse not to think again.

And that is the good news! Later, consensual power politics was to decide that humanity's interests are best served by having three quarters of the world's population undernourished up to and beyond the point of starvation, and by killing many of the remainder with obesity. Can we be sure that it is the fittest specimens who are surviving? But more on that story later.

Meanwhile Frederik is about his task. We have not wasted his time, because he has done that without our help. He is devising a method of writing more than one letter at a time.

At school we all had to 'write lines' at one time or another. Without reference to high or low authority, I guess that today, such practice might constitute 'mental cruelty' or 'infringement of human rights.' When it was accepted procedure, we all tried and failed to hold three or more pencils with one hand and get many lines for the price of one. Frederik's method was a variation on that theme; but it had worse results.

'Fixing a ball-point pen at each end of a twelve-inch ruler with a central 'Master-pen' to operate the ingenious device, the young Strampet's genius came to full fruition when, to overcome the unequal pressure between the central (Master) pen and the outer (Slave) pens he hit upon the brilliant notion of using a thinner writing pad for the inner (Master) copy.'

It was never going to work; he tried anyway. It didn't work! If he could perfect and patent the idea, he could 'clean up.' Come to think of it, it didn't need to work. 'Roll up, roll up! Get your novelty triple writers here, only a tanner each, three for a bob. All my life I wanted to be a barrow-boy, a barrow-boy I always wanted to be.' What would it feel like to be unfettered like that, footloose and carefree? How he longed for a life other than the one he had.

"Who's a cunt?" The uncouth yob's aggressive, snared question came back to him. It was a face he had seen about the town, notable for its ugliness. It had been a nasty moment; three ruffians against two innocents. The two staying instinctively schtum, proceeding along the otherwise deserted road without pause or deviation; they got away with it. Not a time to manifest trace elements of your borderline Tourette's Syndrome which Mozart did or did not suffer from (or enjoy?) because, as it had not yet been invented, he wouldn't have known he had it. In fact, even at that latter time the condition was unheard-of by people generally and unknown to Frederik and the (let us agree) non-Tourette. However, the incident is significant also in that it might have provoked the thought that, in a universal setting the question should not be, "Who's a cunt?" but rather, "Who is not a cunt?" Tricky one that!

At last Frederik produced a letter of moderate neat and tidiness. Folding it carefully, he wheezed a sigh of relief and satisfaction. Better check again for spelling. Smoothing the sheet, his sweaty palm left a grey smudge similar in shape (and to his horrified glance it seemed in size) to Wales. Obscenities jostled their way from his brain to his compressed lips and his mother had switched off the vacuum cleaner just in time to catch his closing expletives. The bedroom door opened.

"Yes, it is sucking grit, I didn't think you'd have

noticed, I don't know how it got up here on the landing, it must have been those men working outside when you were in a hurry and didn't have time to take your shoes off, have you finished your letters?"

"Yes. Nearly."

"Well I won't disturb you, I know you are busy."

Frederik searched frantically for an eraser without success, then realized providence was on his side for once, because with the mark still damp, a rubber would have made things worse. Fresh doughy bread did the trick he had heard, but it gave his father constipation. He knew his mind was wandering but he was desperate. Wholemeal bread would not do, too much roughage, very good for the bowels though, so why would his father not eat it? Simply, because he had always eaten white bread; not because he did not like wholemeal.

Frederik fancied a large slice right then, still warm from the oven with plenty of butter and (with appetite more akin to lust than gluttony) lashings of apricot jam! But he needed to get at least one job application completed before his wife returned, or she would give him hell. She would give him hell anyway (past mistress of 'nagriculture' as she was) and though he stood no chance of securing the position she insisted he apply for; she might not go completely bananas. Oh sod it! Just send the thing as it was, it would make no difference; the envelope might be opened by a lissom young thing, who, perchance would be transported by the smell of his sweat. She might enter (without knocking) the supremo's office and declare, "I sense this epistle to have been dispatched by a great and worthy man. Award him position and power at thrice the salary you were offering and after he has debauched me, slaked his lust on my body and cast me aside, I shall be yours, as you have always wanted, to do with me as you will. I would be privileged and happy to make that sacrifice for so noble a man." It was about his best chance.

CHAPTER FIVE

Prudence turned her head as she crossed the road, a fraction further than was necessary for checking traffic. As she guessed it would be, his face was at the window, low down because he was not dressed. She could have screamed with anger and frustration but when a car travelling faster than she had judged splashed muddy water onto her stockings, she almost cried. His face was docile and questioning. Docile in the popular and incorrect meaning of the word, because he was anything but docile in the true sense, and could be intractable and pig-headed to the point of perversity. Questioning, but with full knowledge of the answers and wishing the questions had not needed to be asked in the first place.

She felt sick and sorry for herself, almost as if she was someone else who had made this grotesque mistake. It was shocking to admit, but it was there in her head and would not be put aside.

People marry for much the same reasons, few in number, some different between men and women, others the same. There is the question, 'why get married' and also 'how did I not see that it would be a mistake;' because divorce figures tell us that for many people, both questions need to be asked.

Simplistic it may appear, but first of all there is the fairy-tale reason; 'and they lived happily ever after.' Next there is the fear of being isolated and alone; exiled from the womb as we are. For men, there is the notion of unlimited sex. For women, unlimited money and unlimited sex, unless of course you are of kingly or aristocratic standing, when naturally you marry for reasons of power, prestige and wealth; having already embarked on the business of living happily, both before and ever after marriage, with whomsoever lovers take your fancy.

From the golden years of Hollywood and onwards, if you are a 'Star' and your price tag needs firming up, you marry whosoever the hell your studio tells you to, or you will not do much more twinkling. But Prudence put those questions to one side as she tackled the immediate difficulties.

At first, she had insisted he should rise first and prepare a modest breakfast, so she could have a little extra sleep. To be fair, he had got up readily enough and gone through the motions, but what to most people is a simple task, was to Frederik, a macabre ritual. He set objects and utensils in place with ceremonial precision, pausing at each movement as if in contemplation. He had dropped plates and pans, he had burned the toast; actual flames, which had set his beard alight as he tried to blow them out and he had trodden on the cat's tail. Insistence that he shave off the beard had cost her clinically diagnosable hysteria.

"You stand little enough chance of getting a job as it is," she had screamed "but with that thing on your face you stand no chance at all."

"Beards are coarse in texture, only because in Western Society, men shave. Arab men never shave from when they are boys, so their beards are soft and silky. I wanted mine to be like that. I never should have shaved."

"What in God's name are you talking about. You are a supposed adult, a grown man with a wife, children and responsibilities. I don't care whether or when you shaved, or saw the light of day for that matter; just get rid of that beard and find a job." Forthwith, she insisted he stay in the bedroom out of her way, while she prepared breakfast herself.

She had wanted children and a social life of cosy, cultured friendliness. Frederik's seemingly mild nature had appeared malleable and probably was so, as far as he could go, but the stop point of his incapability was soon reached and no amount of loving encouragement could move him to higher achievement. She had had complete confidence in her ability to mould him into a suitable husband and father to complement her self-image as a modern, emancipated wife and mother. She had tried and failed.

Had she loved him? If she had, it was love short of what she felt was possible, but that would not have mattered if only he was closer to what she considered to be normal and acceptable. And then there were the twin obstacle tests of all marriages, high-hurdle and pitfall; money and sex. Regarding money, she had long abandoned any expectation of wealth or even modest prosperity. Mere relief from the humiliation of near poverty would have been heaven sent happiness. Both their families were financially comfortable, but in a way that made their own situation worse. Her father's studied non-intervention was perhaps hardest to bear. Outright hostility to his son-in-law just might have spurred him to some sort of assertive action. And her mother-in-law's inability to see fault in anyone, least of all her son, almost moved Prudence to tears of frustration.

So, to Sex. The least said the better perhaps,

considering the present-day propensity to speak about, write about, display, sell and exploit the subject! There can be no avoiding this inescapable matter, though we may dispense with much of the 'graphic detail' the 'earthy realism' and the sheer filth, which has been presented elsewhere. In passing it may be said that without filth we would not know purity.

Let us assist Prudence in her thankless task of rationalizing about sex and marriage, even though for the most part she is not so engaged; she is too busy. Fraught with anxiety, frustrated in her ambitions, she cannot see her situation as, with the benefit of hindsight, we may hope to do.

It has been said, (I concur unreservedly) by the highest (unidentified) Jamaican authority, "Man, a French-letter fuck, not a fuck atarl." So indisputably 'safe sex' is not sex as it should be and that any safety, being only medical and contraceptive, is certainly not safe for the human psyche. This presents us with quite obvious problems, which through the ages have been overcome (to some degree) by variations on the theme of, the 'brute' reproductive urge. For us in the West that urge has always been somewhat circumscribed, by a certain ancient tribe's prohibitions which relate to their population count. Onan might at least have paid her the compliment of spilling his seed on her belly rather than on the ground. If it didn't please the Lord, it would at least have pleased her.

Yes but! No but! The bottom line was and is, that without a fair degree of financial comfort and security, any sexual enterprises, be they of the bedroom, or of the chandelier swinging variety are, long term, doomed. And even then, even then - - but that is another story.

Or maybe fortune smiles on the serene and the well-adjusted, sexually and otherwise; even more perhaps on the culturally unconscious.

Prudence was not given to daydreaming, but she could not help wondering what course her life would have taken, had she not made her first, inevitable mistake; the universal young females' mistake, of giving herself cheaply in the name of romantic passion. Her only consolation was that at least it had not been to a complete nobody. What an actor he had turned out to be. Though acclaimed by both public and critics as his stage and screen performances subsequently were, she was sure his theatrical zenith, was when he had convinced her, she was the object of his undying devotion. When he abandoned her, she was angry and humiliated, but she was now no longer ashamed and disgusted as she had been. His rise to fame and her life as a teacher, wife and mother, now framed a picture she could almost admire. The frame was a la Marc Chagall. The picture itself, changed according to her state of mind. Sometimes Dali, sometimes Beardsley; she open-mouthed and astonished, he demonic, mocking and the incongruous seeming image of a four-year-old Gudrun bereft of her knickers, dancing for them. In that rendering of the image, he was the one with mouth agape.

She thought she had found a way through when she met Frederik, he was a blank canvas; any doubts had to be set aside when she became pregnant. Was it the chicken or the egg? Is ever a woman in such a situation, truly wishing not to be pregnant? It was certain that he needed a firm thrust to activate his momentum, but that this momentum would require permanent and exhausting coercion was something she had not reckoned on. Even so, she could have carried on somehow, had it not been for the betrayal, which had hurt, surprised, but above all angered her.

If it had been with anyone else, she might have been able to overlook it, or if he had been swept away on a tide of passion, but to have it away with her just because she let him, was beyond forgiveness.

As she entered the staff room someone said, "Thank God it's Friday; we are going to the Lake District for the week-end." "Oh, lucky you," someone responded. Their time off is all that concerns them Prudence thought; no wonder the kids never learn anything. She was thankful that as a supply teacher, she had no need to form close relationships with regular staff; they had little in common. She found teaching easy, having as she did, the ability to instil a degree of respect, even fear, in her pupils. She had a crisp, almost forbidding presence.

"Miss!" In the classroom a small child timorously raised her hand.

"I am a married lady; you will call me Mrs. Strampet or Madam. What do you wish to ask?"

"Please may I be excused."

"We have only just entered the classroom, why didn't you go before?"

Knowing that the truth, which was that she was too busy 'mucking about' till the bell rang and it was too late was not required, the child unsuccessfully sought the appropriate answer and only managed, "I forgot Miss."

"Oh very well, but all of you remember, you must accommodate yourselves before coming into the classroom."

"What's accommodate Miss?" a child asked.

"It means have a piss," a boy half-whispered.

Prudence was so demoralised she pretended she had not heard.

She had never entertained much ambition in the field of education, seeing herself rather as the wife of high salaried headmaster, a dilettante influence behind the scenes in a cultural and social role, working as and when required (when she wanted to) on the higher supply teacher rate. How quickly this modest, practical vision had evaporated when she threw in her lot with Frederik. What, in his manner she had taken for judicious restraint masking a reserve of potential and possibility, turned out to be social unease, shyness and insecurity. By then it was too late, she had committed herself to making something of him. Perhaps most important of all he was her (not Gudrun's) 'conquest'. Her success with men had not been resounding, and when Frederik 'went for her' rather than Gudrun she could hardly believe it. A gym teacher with no brains Gudrun slept around and got away with it. No one called her a whore, she was not quite beautiful enough, nor did she engender sufficient envy in women, or desperation in men, to engender that appellation. Women liked her, as well as men. It never occurred to her to ask for money.

It was possible; that was all it was at first, an academic possibility, but the thought had taken on a cancerous expansion. The idea that it had been Gudrun all along; that the pathetic no hoper had lacked the backbone to go for who he really wanted. The thought was excruciating because if it was so, he had got what he wanted by the back door the slimy, duplicitous - - she must not lose control, the class would sense her disquiet - this simply would not do.

Saved by the bell! In this case quite literally Bell, Mr. headmaster, and buffoon.

"Ah, Mrs. Strampet. Glad to have you with us again. It might be for some time on this occasion as Mrs. Blow is away on," (whispered) "maternity - er - well I'm sure you know."

More highly qualified and cleverer than he was, she took mild pleasure in allowing him to display his awareness of those facts.

"As a mother yourself, I thought this might be a good opportunity to introduce the class to some rudimentary sex education. The government is keen to see some initiatives got underway, but does not give us much guidance. It is at the discretion of head-teachers and I wonder if you have any thoughts on the matter, being as you are - err, experienced in - not to say - well you understand my meaning."

"Not entirely," she replied. He was digging himself into a hole and she was not going to help him out. It was well known that after a disastrous marriage he had returned to living with his mother.

"Without wishing to put you under any obligation, I thought if I might observe how you tackle the subject at a most rudimentary - little more than the birds and the bees really, as I said - it would be of great help."

Fast losing patience with his ineptitude she turned from the two conflicting images of his eyes (one through his spectacles) to face the class.

"Who knows why Mrs. Blow will not be with us for a while? Anyone?"

A small boy raised his hand. "Please Miss, my Dad said she's gone up the duff."

"We don't put it quite like that. She is going to have a baby. Does anyone know how long it takes to make a baby?"

"Miss, Miss, Madam! I know, my mum told my big sister."

"Well are you going to tell the class?"

"About two seconds, that's all Miss."

"Not quite what I meant. It takes nine months."

"It takes an elephant nearly two years" chimed the

Bell; looking pleased with him-self now that Prudence had taken the initiative.

"Did anyone notice anything different about Mrs. Blow just before she left?"

"She was sort of giggling."

"Anything else?"

"Miss, she got a new dress - because - because her old one wore out."

"Miss, it was 'cos her belly got fat."

The resulting laughter caused the Bell to chime again with ineffective, "That will do, that will do!"

The look Prudence bestowed upon him said, 'That will do from you as well, thank you.'

"Her abdomen became enlarged because her baby was growing inside."

Partly from relief that arithmetic time was fast being used up and partly from the satisfaction of seeing Ding-dong bettered, the class erupted; mob-like.

"Miss, how can it breathe?" "How does it get out?" "How did it get in there?" "Don't you know that?" "He has to stick his prick in." "It comes out her belly button." "It doesn't, it gets out through her quim." "The doctor has to cut it out, sometimes its dead."

"That will do! That will do! Quiet everyone. I'm

sure we are all grateful to Mrs. Strampet for her lesson. She will answer all your questions after I have gone, meanwhile continue with what you were doing."

Turning to Prudence, his face aglow with relief and confusion the headmaster thanked her. "I think that went very well, so much so I would like you to give the whole school sex while you are here. Excellent, excellent." She did not deign to reply, her look said all she needed as he turned grinning at the door, when it rebounded from his galvanic thrust and struck his elbow.

Prudence faced her class. She was not in the best frame of mind to deal with a subject she was untrained to approach, but at the thought of it being left to someone like the headmaster, she felt constrained to do her best. A small girl raised her hand.

"How *does* the baby get born Miss? Is it through her - he said it's through her belly button."

"I assure you babies are not born that way, through the navel as it is properly called."

"*See*." said the girl, aside.

There was a knowing boy. "Please Miss, how does it start to grow. How does the seed get planted?" The boy was one question ahead; she was not going to fall for that.

"As with any subject, you are not expected to

understand things that are too difficult. You will learn that later, when we do long division. Unless you would like to tackle some long division here and now."

There was, "cor no Miss" and general relief all round.

The children worked well for her. Most teachers threatened what might befall, if pupils transgressed; threats which the children soon perceived to be empty. Prudence left it to their imagination, while she sat reading contentedly. Unusually, that morning, her attention to her book had wavered.

The thought about her husband and Gudrun resurfaced; it was a double whammy. Frederik had got what he wanted, and Gudrun had got the better of her once again. How many times did she need to prove she was the sexy one?

Perhaps in truth, Gudrun was not trying to prove anything.

CHAPTER SIX

Frederik now realised he should never have told her, but at the time it seemed imperative that she should know; it was part of his reason for transgressing in the first place. Between her almost playful interrogation (what a master stroke that had been) and his reckless half-wish to brag, she had extracted a confession. At first she took it (or so he thought) in the spirit in which it was given.

"Was she as good as they say she is?" He had indulged in a smirk, and contributed a rare (perhaps to Prudence his only ever) semi-wisecrack.

"How good do they say she is?"

"So that's how it is, is it?" Uncharacteristically trite words coming from Prudence, the hint of menace in them proved potential for limitless increase.

For a time he walked on air, or the balls of his feet; his heels reluctant to touch the ground. She was quietly subdued, dangerously it transpired, and so he thought, 'This will change,' and it did; it got worse. Though not banished from the matrimonial bed (that would have lacked panache) he was denied all conjugal access, with added cold shoulder emphasis, dispensed with the implacability of death itself.

Her mind now made up, Prudence allowed herself a glimpse back at past experience, not a nostalgic interlude, but a marshalling of resources. She would learn from past mistakes make a new beginning with a man who had some practical ability. Not the sort of ability that Michael had had, which was theatrical, self-serving and cunning. He convinced her he had only three months to live, then, forgetting he had said so, planned their married future together. He had staged a convincing epileptic seizure, hysterical blindness and a fake suicide. None of it worked until he tricked her into getting drunk and more or less raped her. She was seventeen. In those days you didn't tell. Next time they met, he greeted her with maniacal chuckling and gloating. When Prudence told Gudrun what she had done, Gudrun said, "Michael? Oh no I wouldn't let *him*; he loves himself too much!" She had come out on top without trying, or even for that matter, caring.

Frederik went to post the letter. It was not a French letter, he thought. Why could he not focus his mind on what mattered! What *did* matter? What mattered to his wife was clear, but increasingly beyond his capability to provide, but what mattered to him? Nothing! The stark true answer was just that. He wanted to be left alone to dream.

And left alone he was. That night Prudence did not return. He received a message which said, 'I shall be suing for divorce.'

Frederik went to Cornwall in an attempt to ride out the summer scourge of asthma and hayever. Hayfever was a subject for humour, until nearly everyone started to suffer from the complaint and although asthma was never a joke you could say, 'He has asthma,' almost cheerfully whereas, 'She has cancer' you could not; regardless that whichever might kill you, you are just as dead.

Could he ride out his infirmity? Smother him if thou canst, thou pollenous and polluted airs; his scant, shallow breaths shall uphold him. But no, such breathings were as a feather held against a tempest; breathings which initiated the first of his thenceforth annual hospitalisations, which finally terminated his life.

The beach was not crowded, early season absence of most children, a relief to Frederik, who's relating to youngsters, even his own, gave the impression of uninterest. A dog approached, mercifully silent, tail wagging in friendly fashion; it sniffed his leg, and the tail stilled as it turned away. Warmth was becoming oppressive heat and the slight movement of air, was from the land, bringing with it a rich cocktail of pollen. It was the very thing he was trying to escape, his breathing seemed almost antagonistic to his heartbeat, competing for dominance, both insistent on being heard, though otherwise, a strange silence prevailed. At first it seemed like a trick of outdoor sound patterns but soon he had to accept that something unusual was happening. People were talking and laughing silently, they began to rotate, slowly at first and then more quickly with sand, sea and the sun going round, in a world of silence, save for the drumming of his heart.

"Hey man! What you been shooting?" First, the beach had risen; half-filling Frederik's mouth with sand, then there was blackness.

"Was he drowning?"

"No, he just sort of keeled over."

"Only with him being wet I thought he'd been dragged out the sea." The lifeguard breathed a sigh of relief. For a moment he had thought, 'this idiot has got into difficulty while I was been chatting up that brunette in a bikini.'

"No, I think he'd been for a swim; he hasn't moved

so we thought we had better call someone."

"Is this his rucksack? He's one of them hippies been smoking too much of that weed they smoke. Oi mate wake up! I'll be back in a minute there's a young lady over there's been stung by a wasp."

"I don't like the sound of his breathing. He's hardly breathing at all; I think someone should call for an ambulance."

"Isn't there a St. John's man about? I'm sure I saw a St. John's man. I saw one yesterday I'm sure I did. A St. John's man."

Frederik was admitted to hospital, where the staff accepted ultimately, that he had not taken any un-prescribed drugs. They found that difficult to believe, but what they found almost impossible to accept, was that he had taken no prescribed drugs either. Everybody takes drugs, it is almost a matter of honour that you take something to counteract the side effects of the drug prescribed for pain-relief needed after the course of treatment you underwent following your minor exploratory operation.

"Has not your G.P. given you medication for your condition?" asked the nice Indian lady doctor.

"I have stopped going to my G.P."

"Oh, so you attend at the hospital?"

"I do not attend the hospital."

"Why ever not you bad man; don't you know you need to?"

"After so much failure? I prefer to try alternatives."

"Oh, don't listen to those witch-doctors they are not civilised."

He had suffered a physical and psychological crisis; something between what used to be called a nervous breakdown and a mild heart attack, caused by asthma, lawyers, wife, mother-in -law (the latter two virtually 'ex') likewise in-laws generally, the capitalist economy, communist subversion, remnants of repressive sex education, or lack of any such, life as we experience it and other contributing factors.

When he left the hospital in Cornwall, Frederik returned to his parents' home with an acceptance which bordered on contentment. There was some kind of inevitability about it, as if he had never been meant to leave in the first place. He still has some way to go and though his journey through life is now to be mostly downhill, things are not necessarily easier for him. His parents also, bowing to fate; his mother seemingly bathed in uncomprehending acceptance, his father struck dumb by all too comprehending sadness. Coming down from a mountain can be more hazardous than the ascent and though Frederik had never conquered Everest, he had in his own strange way, reached the foothills and looked up. His parents whom he had never thought capable of change, were undeniably in decline. The house they prized as being, 'in one of the better areas,' was rotting around them. They died within weeks of each other, first his mother went without realizing she was going, then his father; fully conscious that there was nothing left to live for.

Frederik's access to his children was to be limited. Apart from legal constraints, he accepted they were for the most part better off with their mother, partly for genuine heartfelt concern for them and partly from sheer laziness; besides which he had almost nothing of a practical or material nature to offer. They knew it to be so and he knew they knew. As for non-worldly qualities such as fatherly feeling, the sharing of individual interests and experience gained by any human, not least one's own father, these were largely lost to them, and to him. If the harsh reality of the domestic set up had not put paid to those prospects, family propaganda would have done so.

He was free again to do as he pleased! But what did

he please? It was too big a question. No one can cope with such a question; far better to be engaged with football pools. He was sure there was a way of out-manoeuvring the promoters. Once he had scooped a vast fortune, then he would think what he wanted to do with his life.

He spent hours poring over the coupons. He assured himself that the money he could so ill-afford to waste was 'investment.'

It had driven Prudence to distraction! Driven her to a point where she could collude with her solicitor and family to brand her husband a pervert.

Pervert (noun) a person whose sexual behaviour is regarded as abnormal. So what is abnormal? Abnormal (adjective) deviating from what is normal. Normal, (adjective). Conforming to a standard. Standard, (noun). We could go on but that would not be normal.

To say that, if we could calculate the total world's populations (past, present and future) we would arrive at the number of different 'normal standards' possible, is asking too much. Or even the number of cultures, races, religions, creeds, nations, movements and sects, from the half-assed to the bloody ridiculous.

So it could be said they were walking on thin ice when they postulated that Frederik was a pervert, merely because they found 'dirty pictures' in his pocket. What right had they, to invade his privacy? Did the lawyer feel smug and superior, knowing he could afford pornography of superior quality? Attitudes changing with time, a Prudence of today, might at the least have need to assert, "He kept wanting me to take it up the Khyber!"

Omnipresent in all ages, pornography, defined as (and I condense) visual, sexual, intended to stimulate erotic (note stimulate, not disgust) has in our age lost much of its clout (forbidden fruit available via television at the movement of a single digit is something to be avoided rather than sought) and has been replaced, in part, by what might be described as 'culinary porn.' Television and the newspaper supplements present a deluge of images and effusions about food and drink. Yesterday's sleazy, record putters on (disk and other riders) have today, been largely superseded, by even more odious, snot-nosed, fast-talking kitchen porters.

Could all of this be a conspiracy on the part of third world countries, to hide the fact that, by eating and drinking less, those who are not actually starving are healthier and happier than their 'envied' counterparts in the West? Or are global economies striving for maximum consumption at maximum prices for maximum profits? Or perhaps an unlikely compact between the two; totally effective in that no one in the 'developed world' (and boy are we developed) seems to mind being urged to rush gluttonously to early immobility. Two systems of population control, starvation and gluttony in contention with, (co-operation even; who knows?) arms manufacture, with its resulting mass slaughter?

But returning to the troubled waters of marriage in general, and Frederik's in particular, an additional problem is, the troubled oil we are wont to pour onto those troubled waters; namely, divorce. Marriage, we expect to be give and take, divorce, is undeniably take and take. In the crudest possible terms, marriage is protection/security (money) in exchange for offspring (sex). Money, a non-negotiable necessity in marriage and a subject for dispute and acrimony in divorce proceedings, it survives as an entity. Sex however, is proscribed after divorce, which surely demonstrates that marriage is a matter of business rather than romance. Even within marriage, sex is at times, an optional entity and utterly worthless (except to procreate) if not by mutual consent, whereas money is a constant constituent.

And besides all that, by timing their divorce near the middle of the twentieth century, Frederik and Prudence let themselves in for a lot of additional trouble. Today, she would merely need to say, 'I wish for a divorce because I am fed up with him and he doesn't make enough money.'

Their children and grandchildren live in a new world where fornication, adultery and pornography (even pornography was not yielding enough profit) have been replaced largely, by drug-induced insensibility! Some of the best parties are experiences you may boast you can't remember anything about. Apparently, the desired way of enjoying sex with a young girl is to drug her to unconsciousness, and be yourself also, as far 'out of it,' as possible. If you are unfortunate enough to be semi-conscious at a 'rave' you can take comfort from the knowledge that even fully conscious you would not be able to speak with, or observe anyone clearly and that whoever you may be touching will not know it is you. Unavoidably of course, you will (together with all souls within a two-mile radius) hear the D.J., but don't be concerned that you have never heard of whoever he declares is 'up from number six.' No one else has either.

Frederik fought many skirmishes with authorities, medical, civil and legal. He seldom won these battles, nor those he should have; those with himself. His parents' house, which he inherited and insisted should be preserved, was at length condemned as unfit for human habitation and demolished, almost about his ears when he still refused to move out. Social Services provided him with hostel accommodation but his absolute unsuitability for communal living was quickly realized. "He's bleeding crackers that one; wants everything done his way but won't do it hisself, oh no; wants someone to do it for 'im if you don't mind!" The tiny council flat he was then allocated could not withstand the negative force of his ineptitude. Within weeks, what had been neat clean and tidy, albeit modest accommodation, was well on its way to becoming the proverbial 'tip.' And true to form, the timing was all wrong. A decade later it could have featured, nay, starred in, that televisual extravaganza 'A Life of Grime' (it was too far gone for 'How Clean is Your House?') Should not these titles be on the lines of, 'How low can standards of television programming sink?' Though granted, there are even worse presentations.

CHAPTER SEVEN

Breathing economically, the visitor, paying his first call to the flat looked around with true astonishment. "Where do you sleep?" he asked. They were sipping Earl Grey in cocktail-party stance (anything resembling a chair was heaped high with rubbish) but no one else being present, without the capacity to mingle.

"Here!" came the slightly surprised answer as, raising a conglomeration of newspaper and rags, Frederik revealed a lower layer of rubbish under which presumably, there was a bed.

"Can you not stay the night?"

"How could I?" It had been his sneaky intention so to do. "I mean, well how could I?"

Even Frederik had to concede that some things are beyond the impossible.

"Could you not sort things out a bit? It is only a minute space after all."

The response shed light on much more than the immediate question.

Frederik's answered, "I could do it if I had a garage."

Although this was some time before his final decline, Frederik could have spoken in similar vein almost any time in his chequered career (the Oxford Dictionary gives two definitions of the word career.)

"Realistically I need three cars," he had said "A Rover for family transportation, a Citroen Utility for easy parking in town and the big Austin for towing a boat."

"But you haven't got a boat!"

"Yes, but if I had a boat."

If I had a boat, if I had a hammer, if I had a perfect profile and a bigger penis. If I had the girl/boy of my dreams; if I had everything I want; but you never will have, so belt up.

Rose was Frederik's last 'fling.' It was not a 'fling' in an energetic sense and if it was 'fling' as in Scottish dancing it was more like an accidental trip-over caused by uneven paving, but they loved with a peaceful fondness compliant with their advanced age; hers well in the vanguard. They had met and their relationship blossomed at Art Classes (concessionary rate fee) Frederik true to form, the lifelong student. Rose was of a refined sympathetic nature and she was able to see less obvious values in people and appreciate different standards of worth.

When the visitor asked 'Why don't you take the quantum leap and live together?' Frederik replied with near indignation, 'I would lose all my benefits!' Rose had a son whose watchful eye on family interests may well have been another consideration and he must surely have been one of the fulsome congregation, who could not put up with Frederik's eccentricities.

He had the wit not to reveal to Rose the chaos of his living accommodation, and she the discretion not to intrude. His domestic conditions were such that no one would or could tackle them, though he maintained personal cleanliness (how he did so was a mystery because the bath was filled with rubbish); and the apartment stank. He would visit her home and in the course of time they enjoyed a compatibility both mental and physical, which Frederik at least had never before achieved.

He missed Rose sorely when she died, it hurt him in a way nothing else had and from then onwards, his decline was inexorable; he felt crushed. She had accepted his shortcomings with good grace, as part of what he was. Not everything in nature is perfect, so why should we expect perfection from human beings who, as part of, but at the same time aside from nature and sometimes anti nature. Mistletoe does not have proper roots of its own, but is not reviled for that reason; even the legless serpent is accepted for what it is.

Frederik was spared the worst of televisions offerings by lack of a receiver, dating from some time onwards after the rot had set in. The rot of course being, round the clock viewing. Did anyone ever really believe entertainment, or even mild interest could be sustained twenty-four a day? He remained faithful to radio; he was Alistair Cooke's most ardent fan. He travelled miles using his buspass to whatever further education course would accept him free of charge. He would lunch at the pensioner's canteen making his way through the town centre, studiously not acknowledging faces he had known all his life. The sustaining of such youthful embarrassments could be regarded as an achievement, but existence in 'real time' walked beside him, never yielding a day.

CHAPTER EIGHT

Inevitably, decomposition had set in, and the stench of the decaying corpse multiplied and then overwhelmed the stink of the filthy flat. It percolated through the cracks at the door and the broken letter box, it ascended to the landing ceiling and beyond to insignificance in the process of global warming, it descended to the ground-floor flats where the never spoken-to neighbour pronounced, "I ain't seen nuffink of 'im for days. I reckon e's croaked."

"Oo you s'posed to tell about a thing like that?"

"Well Council I s'pose, they'll be wanting his flat."

"They are welcome to it and all, the state it's in."

"Did anyone ever come to him like? Anyone you could tell?"

"I think it was his son come now and then."

"Oh, so he has a family."

"Oh yers, and there was someone else come once or twice but last time 'e come, I don't think 'e knew 'im."

"Well I should leave it for now but if that stink gets any worse I shall ad to complain."

This is Frederik's story and that he is deadly departed need not exclude him from playing his part. Being dead was the one excuse he could not use when he was alive. As foil or contributor, it seems proper that, knowing there were times, as with all of us, when nothing happened to him, I should offer conversations we might have had. Perhaps similar conversations that did take place, are on record somewhere. Who knows or remembers?

So look; you are dead and I am in no hurry to join you. The nearest I am prepared to go is to sleep, sleep which in former times caused me concern when it eluded me. The next best thing is boredom. I am trying very hard to be bored; it is not easy. The Russians are very good at being bored. Dostoyevsky, Chekhov were bored, even Tolstoy, though he tried to pretend he wasn't, and the result was wonderful writing. Americans on the other hand, with a few notable exceptions are supreme at being boring. When Ronald Reagan first appeared on the silver screen it was obvious he would never do or think anything interesting in his entire life, but bored he was not; latterly Nancy told him so and he believed her. She was never bored or deflated. O.K. *they* were Joan Crawford, Susan Hayward and Barbara Stanwick, but she was the

President's wife; and that is a big, big deal. She could say so with a straight face on both counts; with little option on one (compliance with popular perception of appropriate U.S. presidential demeanour) and none on the other (tautness of surgically adjusted skin).

John Kennedy was bored with his wife, his mistresses, with unsurpassable, preeminent Office and with his six shirt a day linen change, but he was not boring and for the most part did a good job of appearing to be responsible for social changes that would probably have taken place anyway. George Dubya Bush is not bored and continues the American tendency to switch between showbiz and public life; in his case from third-rate politician, to second-rate comedian.

Russian leaders have tended to be bored, though Putin is showing a worrying tendency towards being interested in world events and 'progress' and his tenacity in holding on to territory which would make a millstone round the neck seem a desirable appendage, rivals that of Margaret Thatcher. (Ref. the Falkland Islands)

In the boring league table, there are those who are beyond the telephone directory, or a badly written biography category, in their lack of capacity to interest us. Take for example (as far as we can tell) Kim Il Sun of

North Korea and certainly our own (or anybody's) Royal family. At least Iddy Amin had the imagination to suggest a union with Princess Anne, which speaks volumes in the defence of our postcolonial foreign policy (it was the British who put him in power) so why did we not call his bluff? Televised, with daily blow by blow account of negotiations (cattle for corgis) it would have been the most successful soap opera ever. Speculation as to who would blink first, would have reached fever pitch and the prospect of Iddy riding to hounds across the English landscape is exactly the image the Countryside Alliance needs to keep people from remembering that however much they say it is the government seeking to ban fox-hunting with dogs, it is actually the will of the British people. It would also have created an opportunity to face the real question behind the hunting debate. Not, is it cruel, but how much enjoyment in the inflicting of cruelty is acceptable? Suggest a frenzied gallop across open country without the prospect of a kill and you will be met with a pitying stare. The idea of hunt saboteurs as quarry might be attractive on the principle of non-contributing creatures needing to be disposed of, so might as well enjoy hunting them down. If hunt saboteurs were in short supply, many old people fall into the same category; useless. The possibilities are endless.

We might discuss the question of cosmetic surgery, (with its proclivity for disrepute) of which, as only getting into its full stride when you took your leave, I feel safe in assuming your experience of breast implants was nil. Let me tell you, you didn't miss a thing. They feel weird! Once you have recovered from the schoolboy thrill of confrontation by two unbelievably large, proudly displayed orbs (not necessarily each at the same altitude) the results are at best disappointing. They feel incongruously hard and cold and only the original areas being sensitive, you may prefer to avoid the silicone. Besides that, anything costing thousands of pounds per handful calls for judicious manipulation. And that's only the recently acquired, competently executed jobs. Happen upon a longer established set of false jugs and you can be in for a nasty surprise. She may need to perform the bra adjustment move (without the bra of course) which can convey an eerie sense that something might come adrift in your hands.

Nose jobs can be more successful, though plastic surgeons are either unaware of, or are withholding from patients the fact that, too deep an upper lip can look much worse than too long a proboscis.

The recent trend towards total depilation, more redolent of meat for carving than flesh for caressing leaves me baffled; not least in that a woman looks less naked with no pubic hair. Notably practised at the decline of the Roman Empire and other times for all I know, I am sure it must denote something of great sociological significance.

We could speak of reality television, except that it is unspeakable and utterly removed from reality and therefore - we could speak of life and -

Why don't you add something? Oh! So you are dead! Excuses, excuses!

CHAPTER NINE

Ronald Strampet had his share of worries. There was the education of his children to think about and also the state of the union; between himself and his spouse that is. The recent drug scandal at his son's school had raised doubts in their minds. Could the boy have been involved? If he was, it might account for the change in his behaviour and unwillingness to communicate with his parents; or was that just part of his 'growing up?' Had the extra drain on their resources of sending him to a private school been worth the effort? His daughter, who he and his wife had always thought of as never likely to cause them heartache, had recently realized she would never be beautiful, in the current, famine victim style. "It is more important to have a beautiful soul," they told her and their consternation at her reply, "Fuck that for a turn-on!" was at least a shared response. He had remembered their wedding anniversary this year and booked a table at a too expensive restaurant. Although dining out was the last thing she felt like doing, she gamely went along with the idea. Had the part time waitress not been an alluring young student, the evening might have been a modest success. He managed to order 'breast of steak' and when his wife, looking motherly, caring and wise (and fat) had said, "It's just your mid-life crisis," he almost struck her.

His career was at an intersection; he could either go up or down and was not sure which was the more frightening prospect. He had to concede that the alarming number of redundancies in the offing represented the worse outcome, that of going down, but in truth that of rising to the responsibility of promotion filled him with almost equal dread. The sudden snatch of the technological world had stunned and stupefied more people than cared to admit. The young go-getters were on the rampage. You were old at forty. They had a sneering, confident mien, which imputed, "I am riding high! That's right, I'm on cocaine, what are you going to do about it, *Asshole*!" He had coped so far, but only just, and the seductive prospect of early retirement which, lately had insinuated its way into his thinking, had taken a severe bruising from the apparently imminent collapse of his pension fund society.

The family property he was staining every nerve and sinew to pay for, (with a view to selling later at a considerable profit) was still not out of negative equity.

Any sentence with the word 'equity' induced a cold sweat, (referencing obliquely as it did, his failing pension fund society) and the thought of costs when his father might need to be put into a care-home, was daunting.

He was travelling by train because the second car (his wife said she would need the first car) was being serviced; well expensively repaired actually, because owing to indifferent maintenance, the cam belt instead of being renewed (as it should have been) had broken, causing considerable damage. Nowadays you could not call a spade a spade, so when his local mechanic and 'character,' jack of all trades was unable, indeed unaware of the need to do the job, he was denied the satisfaction of saying the fellow was 'simple minded.' Just as you could not say of a government minister who had awarded huge contracts to a company and then left office to join that company, "He is a crook!" Well you could say so, but few would take heed because so many were attempting to do something similar. It was standard practice for managing directors to negotiate contracts which, however miserable a failure, would not compromise their extortionate bonus. Political parties could safely draw up manifestoes, which they had no possibility or intention of fulfilling, because the smart brains behind the (hopefully) electable front men know that political persuasion is ultimately not a matter of reason, but of temperament and inclination.

The slow train stopped at every station, which would not have mattered had Ronald not been saddled with a cheap-suited man sitting opposite who wished to display his possession of and disguise his lack of need for, a laptop and a mobile phone. The great communication revolution was underway, further isolating person from person and individuals from their true selves.

"Hi, it's Simon. - Simon Green. I'm on the train trying to catch up on a backlog of - sorry - Simon Green - Oh I thought I was speaking to - that's right - in a meeting. Oh no problem, no problem - he's got my mobile number - thanks, not at all, no problem."

The man switched his attention to the laptop, his heavy hands punishing the keys in an unconscious parody of Miss Remington; a transsexual grotesque from the nineteen fifties. His 'mobile' addressed its puerile signal to the travelling public with blissful assurance. His face lit up.

"Hel' - no I hadn't forgotten. Was it pork and beef or just pork? - No don't wait, they might ask me to - err, I suppose I shall have to take them for a drink after. I must go I'm expecting a very important call. Yes, alright. Yes

ALRIGHT!" He sighed a sigh of the stressed-out, overworked executive he hoped to become and returned his attention to the computer. He jabbed, it bleeped plaintively. He jabbed again. It sulked for a while; then bleeped twice.

Ronald Strampet's conscience was not entirely clear. He knew he should visit his father more often, but it was such a daunting task, the intervals between visits were getting longer and more laden with guilt. That his father was in a sense blameless only made matters worse; he made no demands and accepted his role as second-class parent and grandparent, without complaint. Why did he not make some effort to assert his natural rights? Surely things would be easier if he did so. Was there some dread malfunction in root and branch of the family tree? Why could not his father maintain at least a minimum standard of household cleanliness and order? It was a subject upon which his mind would not properly come to bear. His mother's mental habit of cancelling his father out of existence was by association, partly his also and too entrenched to dispel. The conditions of his father's life were something left apart, not confronted, un-discussed, silently festering.

The train reached his destination at last and rather

than take a taxi, Ronald decided to walk the mile or so to kill some time. It was cowardly and he knew it, but he needed to think how he might broach the subject of some change in his father's domestic arrangements. Perhaps he could persuade him to one more attempt at some form of communal living. Who was it said 'hell is other people'? Maybe that is true. Certainly, he himself would not relish the thought of sharing his time and space with others who would be either equally reluctant, or only too eager to invade his privacy. As he reached the small apartment building, he admitted to himself that he would probably fudge the issue once again and avoid the old man's distress and indignation. Entering the bleak hallway, he was aware of the dank odour of damp concrete. A door opened suddenly and was closed furtively, the familiar musty, gingery, vaguely urinal smell was today augmented by something different; an odour his mind placed in parenthesis as he ascended the cold steps to the first floor. After locating his key in the lock, he paused for a while before entering the flat. His father preferred not to arouse the unwanted attention of the neighbours by a knock, or undue announcement of arrival. No one other was in possession of a key. He opened the door softly and soft came the realisation that his father was dead. 'Problem solved' passed through his brain, concurrent with his shame for the thought. The stench was beyond nauseating, it was elemental; almost creative in its intensity. It did not lead to the body, it *was* the body, encompassing the space. Entering the tiny bedroom his gaze, unerring, met the rotting corpse. Not only did the loud winged and writhing mass deny it was a figure at rest, it was huddled pathetically, between a broken chair and the riven bed. He stood, outside of time looking down. A voice inside him spoke. "This is disgusting; please get up. I am your son. You are my father."

Printed in Great Britain
by Amazon

83498271R00072